AF488562

GRAY WOLF
BLOOD TRAIL

RAY ROWAN

For information contact: info@outlawspublishing.com
Cover design by Outlaws Publishing LLC
Published by Outlaws Publishing LLC
November 2024
10987654321

CHAPTER ONE

The year of 1868 had marked the end for many of the Great Plains wars as the native inhabitants surrendered. Starvation, loss of hunting grounds along with the depletion of the bison herds had pushed the people of the land to the brink of their existence. Having lost the wars to the settlers with their lands being put under the plow. Their hunting grounds now being fenced off and turned into pasture land for sheep, cattle, along with herds of horses. Where buffalo had once roamed freely were now partition homesteads.

This spiritual animal which had covered the land in times past held the life of the native people within it once mass herds that had counted into the millions had now been reduced near the point of extinction. This life sustaining animal had supplied every aspect of the native inhabitant's life spiritual, nourishment, clothing, as well as the hide used to make their portable homes.

They had fought other tribes over the course of history for this land but this new invader was different. There seem to be no limit to their numbers. A hundred could be killed and two hundred more would come. The Kiowa had been vastly reduced and could no longer sustain the losses. The Kiowa along with the other tribes had no choice but to sign a forced peace treaty as a defeated people. This systematic system had been slowly moving the native people out of their land for the last 50 years, but had taken on steam after the end of the Civil War and the railroad pushing its way across the Great Plains connecting the Eastern with the Western part of this now growing country. Leaving no place for the once free people of the land or their sacred animal. Left with no choice but to sign their life, land, and freedom away. The great chiefs worn down and most of their once proud warriors were dead, starving, or weakened by tainted water supplies found along the way had no choice but to accepted the terms given to them.

The Great leaders had, Gray Wolf had not, he knew this was his land and he was going to stay here until he said otherwise and no army officer, or great man of Washinton was going to tell him otherwise. He made his own decisions and he had made it.

The Kiowa Chiefs had signed the peace treaty and the people were being rounded up to head out to the appointed lands of Oklahoma and Ohio as well 'most' had anyway. Gray Wolf refused to submit and was being hunted by the pony soldiers. For days now he had been on the run as he had left the allotment group he had been assigned to. Having left with only the deer skin pants, shirt and moccasin's he had on. Easily getting past the guards on second watch as it had been a moonless night.

By daybreak, more than a dozen mounted troopers were on his trail. But after no more than a hundred yards the trail vanished and they had to turn around to gain help from a Pawnee scout. The scout picked up the trail after looking around for a half hour. Leading them out at a snail's pace as he slowly made his way forward leading them in a North Eastern direction which at first puzzled the soldiers. Not the scout, smiling as he looked towards the mountains. He knew Gray Wolf well enough to know no one was going to catch him or force him back if he did not wish to go. This was going to be risky chasing that Kiowa.

"What do you think White Hawk, I mean really think?" Sergeant Mason asked as he watched him looking toward the mountains.

"I think that Kiowa will kill us all and shoot the Sergeant in the head. He is going to the mountains. There are many caves, easy to get lost. If you follow him into the mountain trail it will flow with blood."

"Oh, I see," the Sergeant responded. "But he has no gun to shoot anyone, no food, knife, horse, or heavy clothing, no supplies."

"A Kiowa can drink the blood of a snake for his water, eat bugs under the rocks, and make weapon from many things. But maybe he plans to catch a fish in a shallow stream, or steal what he needs along the way."

"White Hawk, he could, I guess If we give him time to stop. I have no plans of letting him slow down long enough to catch a fish. I am going to push him until he drops. If he eats, it will be grubworms or snails out from under the rocks. So how far ahead do you think he is?"

"Hard to tell as his tracks are very hard to read. He hides them well, only a damp toe print, a broken stick or a broken blade of grass is only sign to follow."

"White Hawk, we have been at this for hours and not much daylight left and I can still see the line from here. We have not covered more than three hundred yards over the whole day. We need to move back and pick up here at daybreak. Won't be hard to located with the buzzards circling ahead, the smell of something dead hangs in the air."

"Yes, we will move around that as Gray Wolf would not be there."

"Why do you think that Sergeant?"

"Why would he? No reason for him too. A dead animal is of no use to him."

"No Sergeant, I guess he would not, but I do not understand how he vanished that quick. It is almost like the ground opened-up and swallowed him."

"White Hawk, Gray Wolf is hiding his tracks, but he cannot dig a hole to hide or we would have found the fresh dug dirt. No, he is up ahead watching us, somewhere. I do not understand why we have not spotted him. But he is there, has to be as there is no way for him to travel very fast on foot as he is. Tomorrow is a whole new day and we will come back here with a fresh start."

Marking the spot and moving back to the line as they sat up camp. The Kiowa women stopped to build fires and cook as the night rolled in. Sergeant Mason ordered his men to set guard of two men on each watch which would last two hours each. With plans to move out at daybreak. The renegade must be brought back into the line.

White Hawk and Sergeant Mason sat down on a saddle blanket to eat as they discussed the day's activities. "What do you thing he is going to do White Hawk? Where do you think, he is going to go? Really, when you get down to it, what can he do, he is walking with no supplies, no horse, food, or even a knife. By now he is hungry, tired, and it would be my guess that he is about ready to give it up and walk back into camp."

"Sergeant, I am not sure, but hungry he is not as he will eat things you would not. When hungry, he will pull up rocks to eat things found there, rocks can be used to kill a bird, or he could steal a pig from a nearby farm. No, he is not hungry, or won't be for long. As for a weapon, he will find a way, most likely from a local planter. No, I believe by daybreak, he will have stolen a horse, have food extra, and a weapon to get by with. Tomorrow will be a whole new day and as we sleep, he will have spent the night getting things he needs to survive. No, he will find a way Sergeant. Gray Wolf may do a lot of things, coming back in is not one of them, not alive anyway."

"You really believe all of that don't you White Hawk? Why?"

"Because that is what I would do Sergeant. He has considered all of this before leaving, no, he will not come back."

"What about sleep; he should be tired and needing to rest as he had been on the move the whole day. Even the mighty Gray Wolf needs to sleep."

"Sergeant, he will sleep a couple of hours and use the night to gather the things he needs. Although you can be sure by now, he is a long way from here. He is trying to gain as much ground from here as possible. Yes, he is on the move, quietly taking what he needs from a local planter, by daybreak, someone's horse, pig, and weapon left out will be missing. He will be moving for the mountains or someplace he knows well. Could be most anywhere as Gray Wolf could fit in as he knows how to live in the white man's world."

"Why do you think that White Hawk? He is a Kiowa."

"I know that, he spent a lot of time as a boy around your people. He learned to trade, live, and speak the language. His sister did as well and married a white homesteader."

"You speak of him as if you know him, White Hawk, how do you know so much about Gray Wolf? He is your enemy, not your friend."

"That is true, but I spoke to the Kiowa women; they told me this. They speak of him around the campfires, they call him 'Gray Wolf' because like the wolf, he moves with ease, hunts' unmercifully, and can seemly disappear into the night. No, in their words he will not be caught. With him you should expect the unexpected, plan for the impossible, and prepare to die if you cross him."

"What does that mean, are you afraid of him?"

"No, I am not, but tracking a ghost will be a little harder than tracking a man. Ghosts leave no tracks. Wolves are like smoke in the night; you see them when they want you to."

"White Hawk, he is a man, he is not a wolf, ghost, or smoke, he will leave's tracks, he bleeds, and breathes like any other man, like you or I; he can die. Get me close enough and I will prove it. A ghost he will be, filled with lead. Yes, I will make him a ghost after we find him. But right now, I am tired and we need to get some sleep, Tracker we have a ghost to catch tomorrow" the Sergeant responded as he dumped his coffee and headed to his tent.

Looking around at the dozens of cooking fires which were starting to die down and most everyone was bedding down as the day had been long and hot. Making the journey that much harder as they carried, pulled, or pushed along the few things carried with them on their march to their new homes in Indian territory which is in Oklahoma. The long march had been brutal on the other tribes and will be no less so on the Kiowa. Losing many before reaching the trails end. Having been given the name 'Trail of Tears' by the Cherokee in in 1838. Forced from all that they knew, having to leave the land that they loved for unknown territory which is why some like Gray Wolf fought back.

Walking into his tent, Sergeant Mason pushed off his jacket and boots and quickly laid down. The day had been hard, hot and chasing some fool Indian that refused to follow the rules made it all that much harder. No matter, he will be brought back in by tomorrow, he is going to his new home. Thinking, if he does this again after we get him back, he will be shot, I will make sure of that. Then he drifted off into a heavy slumber.

Hours later, he woke up to screams and shots fired, 'Fire' "the wagons are on fire," could be heard as he glanced around in confusion taking a moment to wake up. Rubbing his eyes as he tried to focus, reaching up to turn up the oil lamp that was hanging above him in his tent. Sitting up as he glanced over at his pocket watch 2:15. "Why do these things happen in the middle of the night?" he said to no one as he pulled on his boots. Quickly running out of the tent and looking around. A couple of supply wagons were on fire as soldiers tossed buckets of water on them. Loose horses ran around as some tried to round them up.

"What in thunder is happening?" Sergeant Mason screamed out to a private as he ran by.

"Sir, I am not sure, I was awakened by all the commotion and I am trying to help."

About that time, one of the night guards came by and heard the questions. "A couple of horses were taken from the Picket line Sir."

"Who the blazes are you!" Sergeant Mason screamed out?"

"Wagon Master Deeds, Sir. on night duty," he said as he saluted.

"Who took the horses, did you see them?"

"No sir, too dark and it happened so fast. Most likely a renegade Sir."

"Okay, carry on and go help put out those wagons." Get those fires out."

"Yes Sir," he said as he saluted and turned away.

Looking around, things seemed to be getting back to normal as the fires were being put out and the horses were rounded up, the Sergeant watched some of the Indian women that had come out to see what was happening as they seemed nervous about something, but he was not sure what to make of it. He could not see anything they were doing other than looking around. Anyway, everything seemed to be back under control, for now as he headed back to his tent to lie back down and salvage as much of the night as possible before daybreak.

Quickly falling back asleep, daybreak came fast as he awakened to the trumpet call of reveille awaking the troops, and others as well. Reluctantly, he sat up and again pulled on his boots. Standing up as he could hear the men talking outside of his tent. "How many do you think he got?"

"How many who got what and what did they get?" He asked as he pushed the tent flap back.

"Horses Sir, someone stole a couple of horses and we think a few things were taking from the supply wagons as well." A young corporal answered. Which had been walking by, as he quickly saluted the Sergeant.

"Do you have any idea who did it?"

"No Sir, not yet anyway."

"Very well, carry on Corporal," he barked out.

The corporal quickly saluted and walked away.

Walking over to the mess wagon as he grabbed some coffee, ham, and eggs, the Sergeant sat down on a camp stool and sluggishly ate as he considered the possibilities of what had taken place. The men standing around with each giving a different opinion of who it may have been.

"Purely speculation Sir, as no one saw anyone and not sure if anything was taken from the supply wagons as there is no way to tell from the fire damage done." Private Thomas said as he saluted and walked up to get some coffee.

"What did you say Private?"

"Sorry Sir, it is that you seemed to be in deep thought. Four wagons loaded with supplies was burned or have fire damaged."

"Private, are you suggesting the fire was set intentionally?"

"Yes Sir, I am, to cover the tracks of whoever stole from them."

"Well, we could go from group to group until we found the supplies."

"No sir, I don't believe any of them took it."

"Then, who could it have been then?"

"A renegade Sir."

"You mean to tell me, a renegade walked up here last night with several guards on duty, stole two horses and helped themselves to our supplies without anyone knowing. Then on top of it all, set a fire to cover his handy work."

"Yes Sir, that is about right."

"What do you think about the fires last night White Hawk?" Sergeant Mason asked as he watched White Hawk come up for a cup of coffee.

"I think we will have a hard day catching Gray Wolf as he now has a horse and supplies."

"'Gray Wolf, do you really think he would have enough brass to try to get back into camp after leaving it?"

"Yes, I think maybe it was him playing with the Sergeant. Did you feel a hand touch you in your sleep, like a wolf; he moves in silence, takes what he wants, and no one sees. I think much trouble hunting Grey Wolf, camp women say he cannot be caught. He is like smoke; you may see him, but can never get your hands on him. That is how he came back to camp, guards could not see him, cannot shoot smoke, smoke cannot be seen in the dark. That is what women say."

"White Hawk, not only are we going to get our hands on him, but we are going to smoke him out of the hole he hides in. We will get smoke, then you will know it is only foolish superstition. Gray Wolf can be seen like anyone else; bullets can clean his hide; I will get my hands on him and squeeze his neck as I put him in irons for transport over to the government promise land. I do not understand why so many do not want to go as they have land and government issued supplies."

"Land, no good, no game, Kiowa do not plant. Women say Grey Wolf will not go and pony soldiers will never catch 'Great Smoke'. He is like the air, you know he is here, you can feel him, smell him, but you will not be able to catch him."

"White Hawk, we will see," Sergeant Mason said as the men rode up ready to start the day.

Private Layton handed over the reins to the Sergeant's horse that he had saddled up and brought in. "Thank you Private, now we have a renegade to track down!" Sergeant Mason screamed out loud enough for the words to be heard across camp. Looking around for White Hawk which had already left camp and headed out to start hounding the trail. White Hawk wasted no time as they picked up where they had stopped the day before.

Following close behind, the Sergeant watched as White Hawk slowly moved as he crawled close to the ground looking for turned stones, broken leaves, or a print in the ground. Then, he suddenly stood up and ran without bothering to follow any tracks. Running for several hundred yards as he then stopped and circled widely before he ran forward. The tracks of two horses could be clearly seen as he followed the trail. Running with Sergeant Mason and his men following close behind waiting for his signal for them to move ahead.

"What do you think White Hawk, is he close?"

"No, he was here before daylight as the tracks are wet with the morning dew. We are many hours behind him, but should be able to get close as he is leading a supply horse."

"Supply horse? So, it was Gray Wolf that hit us last night. What supplies could he have? A couple of horses, some grain, and maybe a coat."

"The tracks of the horses are deep and he is moving slow. Which means they are both heavily loaded and he is not worried much about any that may follow. Could be he wants to be sure you do. Gray Wolf has everything he needs; the fires was set to keep the guards busy as he found things he wanted. He has enough supplies to winter in if needed, the pack horse alone would keep him enough meat for three fortnights. But most likely he could hunt for enough meat to survive. See these tracks here?" White Hawk said as he pointed to them. "These are where he stopped, tracks of both horses, his shoe prints are where he walked some, leading them and the square mark here is where he leaned on his rifle as he stopped to look around. He did this to let you know he is armed now."

"Rifle, he has a rifle? How? Having the horses along with stolen supplies maybe, but a rifle, no one reported missing one. We are now dealing with a renegade that is fully supplied. How on earth could he have marched into a well-guarded camp, raided two supply wagons, stole two horses, and helped himself to a rifle from the tent of a sleeping personnel?"

"The fires Sir, that is why he burned the wagons to draw away the attention." Private Thomas responded.

"Yes Private, you are right, but how could we have not seen that coming?"

"Sir, most of the ones that have managed to escape keep going and run until they are caught. It seems to me this renegade has different plans. He knew he would need the supplies for a long-term escape plan and as you said Sir, he has brass. He is leaving tracks almost seemly daring us to follow."

"White Hawk, you said that he could vanish if he wanted to, why is he leaving clear to follow tracks now after making it so hard to find them yesterday?"

"Yesterday he had no horse, now he wants the Sergeant to know that he has what he needs and is going to fight. He will not give up and will fight to the death if pushed. But I, also, believe he wants us to follow for the moment. He is clearly heading to the mountains or he wants us to think that as he may leave a clear trail leading there and then change after he has us following a false trail that leads to the mountains as he heads out in a different direction. I believe he is setting the course for that as that is what I would do. But hard to say about Gray Wolf, he might go up into the mountains to vanish into some hidden cavern that only he knows about as there are a lot of them up there some large enough to hide the horses in."

"We'll follow fast and push him hard. Clear tracks mean we can easily trail him on the run." Sergeant Mason said as he went around White Hawk. His troops followed close behind as White Hawk watched him ride away. Riding fast through the now gathering brush, trees, and low-cut tree stumps. Pushing hard the Sergeant did not see the rope stretched across the trail as he ran face long into it. Throwing him off his horse along with two others that were following close behind. White Hawk running close behind the end of the group could only hear the screams as they hit the ground.

"As I was saying, I do not think I would get into a big hurry as that may be what he wants you to do," White Hawk said as he walked up in time to help the Sergeant up from the ground. "He could be setting a trap for you. I believe I would slow down and be careful with Gray Wolf as he has been known to pull this kind of trickeries." White Hawk said as he cut down the rope stretched across the trail. Before he could say another word, a shot rang out as a bullet hit the ground beside Private Thomas. They all jumped from their mounts and laid flat on the ground as they tried to find out where the shot had come from. After several minutes, no other shots were fired.

"White Hawk, I would say this would make a good place to camp out the night as you scout ahead to see if you can locate him as we set up camp. The men have not stopped all day and they need the rest after eating in the saddle. Besides, I think I cracked my back with that fall."

Without saying a word, White Hawk, disappeared through the brush. Easing through the heavy brush in hopes of maybe finding Gray Wolf, but knowing he would not as he had used the shot to cause them to hunker down and it had worked. Giving him time to rush out as they had most likely come up faster than he had thought they would.

Sergeant Mason had the men get the fires started and coffee on by the time White Hawk came back for his report. He could smell the meat cooking as he rounded the trail. "Find anything?" the Sergeant asked as he walked up."

"Found where he hid and took the shot at the camp. Also, where his tracks headed out on down the trail. Most likely, not far ahead watching the smoke from the campfire as he sets up his own camp. But an early start may help us gain time on him."

"Why do you think that White Hawk?"

"Because the horse he rides has a loose shoe and there is nowhere around here to get it fixed."

"Since when did that matter to a renegade, they don't shoe their horses?"

"Yes, that is true, but the pony soldiers do and the horse was stolen from your camp. He will need to get it off or fixed as the horse is limping because of it. He will not get far very fast."

"White Hawk, sit down and have something to eat, we can catch him at morning light. That horse may be his undoing, stealing from the army. I knew it wasn't going to take very long to catch him as it never does. I have never taken more than a few days to round one up. Gray Wolf is no different, we will have him tied to a horse and on the way back within a day or so. Then by a handful of fortnights we should be getting the group close to their new home in the Oklahoma territory."

The night grew dark as the fires grew low. A bottle came out from somewhere as each took a small sip from it as it was passed around. "Easy on that bottle Private, you have guard duty in a couple of hours." The Sergeant said to Private Johnson as he took too long a sip from it.

"Yes sir, just a little too warm my bones as it gets cool later."

After a few sips the Sergeant and his men leaned back and started to close their eyes. White Hawk found a spot to bed down over by the warm fire as he pulled the blanket over his head to block a mosquito that was bothering him.

CHAPTER TWO

Gray Wolf, had started out with every plan to follow the peace treaty that had been signed by the chief. Having been a tracker during the war for the North, he believed he would be excluded from this scourge. But as the Blue Bellies came into the village and starting rounding up the women and children, he watched as they pushed them from their wigwams, giving them only minutes to get ready for the move. Then herding them out like cattle being moved for the slaughter as they pushed them from sun-up to sun-down. He had decided he was not going to leave his homeland where as a child he had grew into a man and his aged parents had died here. He would die here as well.

After a few nights to figure out the guards, the time schedule for the pony soldiers, and when would be the best time to ease out, he decided around the second watch as they changed guards which would be the best time to try. To his amazement, it had gone smoothly with no one noticing as he placed a gray army blanket over his body to help cover the movement and crawled out. After leaving the camp, he ran until daylight to get as far away as possible and only then did it occur to him that there was no way he could last for long. He had left without a weapon, supplies, or a horse.

Having ripped and tied a large part of the blanket to the back of each of his moccasins to drag and help cover his tracks as he walked. He knew they would be on his trail as soon as it was discovered that he had left. Using rocks, falling trees, and any hard surface to walk on that would help to conceal his having passed. The early morning had been dark and hard to make time as seeing had been difficult and now a new problem had arisen. His stomach was empty. Deciding on a change of plan as he looked for a place to hide until the day was spent. But where, the pony soldiers would find him quickly now that it was breaking daylight.

It was then that he noticed buzzards circling. Moving quickly and heading toward where they were at eating a wild horse that had died. Not liking his plan, but it should work to keep the soldier boys and their Pawnee tracker away. To be double sure, he broke off a small bush and moved back to rake out any tracks he may have left for the last 100 feet and then walking backwards, he brushed out his trail. After making sure they were brushed out, he rushed back over to the carcass Quickly, digging out from under the carcass to create enough room for himself as he placed what was left of the blanket above him under the carcass and pulling in enough dirt to cover himself up under the dead horse. Above he could hear the buzzards picking at the carcass as he attempted to cover his nose with part of the blanket and try to get some rest. but by next daylight if all went as planned, he would have a full stomach along with supplies. He could afford a few hours of rest. Sleep did not come easy, but after a while he was exhausted enough and sleep did come.

Hours later, he was awakened by rough movement of the carcass being pulled, by most likely, hungry coyotes. Quickly pushing himself out as he swung his arms wildly to scare them off. It worked to a point as they stepped back a few feet, but not ready to give up their meal. Gray Wolf did not try to back them off and quickly made his way back toward the camp as he had slept the whole day. The night being moonless with stars blinking by the millions he could easily see the fires of the camp guards lighting up the silhouette of the wagons and tents in the dark background.

Running for well over an hour as he made his way back to the encampment, Gray Wolf worked on a plan as he circled the outer edges of the camp. Looking around in the camp a canopy of smoke hung over the area as the fires burned low. The three guards on duty seemed to be more concerned with watching the sleeping natives. Most likely to be sure no one else slips out into the night. For a few moments, Gray Wolf held some remorse for having put extra pressure on his people due to his own escape. But he had no plans of giving up, quite the opposite, as it had hardened his resolve to prove to the Troopers that one Kiowa could out best them along with their Pawnee scout. But to do this, he needed a horse, possibly two as one would be needed to carry the supplies which he would need for a long stay in the upper elevations of the mountains which is where he would need to escape to. Once there, he would not be found as the old ones had shown him places that no Pawnee tracker could ever find or even know about.

Taking far more time to reach the camp than he had wanted, he wasted no time as he looked for the weak spot to enter the camp. Looking around toward the center of the camp, Gray Wolf spotted what he assumed was the Pawnee Scout sleeping close to a group of troopers. "I will teach you to follow me, you blue dog. They have taken our land, but they will never take our heart. I am going to make you and those who dare to follow me pay. They will remember me and tell the stories of this around their campfires." He quietly whispered to himself.

He desperately needed a horse and supplies. But there seemed to be no way to get past the three guards. One or two yes, but three would be hard to work past. Then he noticed Summer Rain step out to most likely find a place to relieve herself. All three soldiers stopped to watch this young Kiowa maiden as she was very easy to look at. An idea quickly came to mind if he could get her to help him. Quickly moving around to catch her as she moved to the edge of camp. She had picked a heavy growth of pinyon trees. Watching her disappear into the shadows of the night, Gray Wolf quickly made his way around to the grove of trees, and quietly called out her name. "Summer Rain, can you hear me?"

"Yes, who is it?"

"Summer Rain, it is me Gray Wolf, I need your help."

"Help? I thought you were long gone, word around camp is that the soldiers hunt for you."

"Yes, they do and that is why I need your help."

"What can I do, I am only one and I have no weapon?"

"Summer Rain, you hold far more than you realized, the guards, they watch you. You can keep them busy watching you as I take what I need." They had not noticed, but others were already there as it was the most private place available., Morning Sun and Little Elk which heard the conversation as they sat quietly.

"Gray Wolf, we will help; how long do you need?" Little Elk responded?

"Who is this?" Gray Wolf asked?

"Friends that will help you, go, do what you must, we will keep them busy."

With that said, Gray Wolf hurried away disappearing into the night as he eased around to where the horses were corralled by rope and wagons. As he reached the horses, he noticed the supply wagons pulled together not more than 50 feet away. Easing there first as he pulled up the canvas covers to find the supplies needed. Quickly looking around to see where the guards were, they were busy watching the girls. Which by now had come out to the edge of camp on the far side, pushing each other as they seemed to argue about something as Summer Rain stood nearby. She watched as Little Elk pushed Morning Sun to the ground and pull her braids. Morning Sun screamed as if in pain and threw a wild punch toward Morning Sun. They held the guard's full attention.

In the meantime, Gray Wolf wrapped up three large bags of supplies along with several boxes of ammo and a rifle he found standing close by a tent. Easing back around to the horses, he took his time as he bridled one horse and tied a rope around the neck of another. Easing them out toward the supply wagons as he moved around tents filled with sleeping troopers. Gray Wolf tied the supplies over the pack horse along with his newly secured rifle and eased them out of camp. Once out of camp, he tied them off and eased back in. After reaching one of the supply wagons filled with barrels of coal oil for the camp lamps, he opened the valve to one of the barrels to let it slowly run as he tossed a match onto it. Running out of camp as he looked back to see it slowly build up and to his amazement, the guards had not noticed it. The girls held their total attention. But someone back in camp screamed, 'FIRE!' as the whole camp quickly came alive.

Gray Wolf rushed out into the night with his horses and supplies. Quickly making his way out to a safe distance, he mounted and rode away into the night. Occasionally looking back as the fire now grew lower as it is most likely being brought under control by the panic troopers. Riding for the next three hours as daylight broke. He stopped to quickly eat some dried beef that he had liberated from the wagon. He washed it down with a canteen he had found hanging from a tent which he had taken it from. As a matter of fact, he had taken three filled with water, a few tools he had found, along with a hat that would come in handy as the day heated-up. Smiling as he considered by now, they had figured it out that he was the one that had boldly gone back into camp and liberated a couple of horses and burned a supply wagon, possible more as it spread. Old Captain Lane, and Sergeant Mason will be gunning for me now. "Crafty Indian," is a term the sergeant would not use, but that is what I am," Gray Wolf said out loud as he smiled. "I am going to show that Pawnee some new tricks, never learned, or taught to him. Then I may kill him or give him a mark to carry and remember me by."

With daylight breaking, That Sergeant would be mad as a hornet won't wait for full light, he is coming. How far back on his trail the troopers were, is hard to say but they are there. Slowly making their way across the open space. Now to block out my trail, to slow down that Pawnee bloodhound. Finding a narrow pathway, he tied a rope about neck high above the trail and rode out a couple of hundred yards and waited on top of a rock. He did not have to wait long before he spotted dust rising in the distance and took a blind shot to slow them down and to his surprise someone fell. He jumped on his mount and rode hard for an hour until his mount started to limp. Stopping to have a look, it was a loose shoe. Luckly, he had brought along a set of plyers and he quickly removed all four from each horse and packed them away in a gunny sack to keep that Pawnee guessing. It was then he spotted the bird nest. I'll give that old crow bait something to sniff at," he whispered as he smiled. Looking around for a stick long enough to fit his need. After having found it, he quickly dug out a hole a foot deep or so and then carved out an elongated hole the length of the stick. He then took the empty bird nest and attached to the end of the stick with a strip of leather string. Then placing it inside of the hole with the nest sitting down in a carved out shallow hole to fit its size. He quickly made sure about a foot of the stick was over the larger hole, so when stepped on it would spring up and toss the nest into the air. Simple, but effective.

As expected, the horses dropped out some fresh offerings as they grazed. After using a large piece of tree bark to shovel up the contribution of horse manure. He filled the bird nest to overflow, covering the outer edges. He quickly placed sticks, grass and leaves over the hole along with a little dirt to help conceal it. The trap-door when stepped on will give that Pawnee something to make the flies happy for the rest of the day. Hopefully slowing him down as he will be busy looking for other surprises set in his path.

Laughing as he considered the thought of that army dog cleaning the horse manure from his face if all went as it is supposed to. He could count his lucky stars, "I am not ready to rid myself of him, 'yet' as those traps can be deadly if set with pointed sticks." Quickly pulling the horses from the grass they had been so involved in as he mounted up and spurred his mount forward with the pack horse following close behind. Looking back, he could see a flock of birds being pushed from their rest as something frightened them most likely the troops tracking him.

Riding hard for the next hour to gain distance between himself and those that pursued him. Gray Wolf slowed to let his mounts catch their breath as they were lathering up and breathing heavy. As he did, he rode up on a small stream and he could see downstream there was a small cabin with a horse and a cow penned up. "Horse, we don't need any trouble from them old boys," stepping down as he talked to his mount. "We will quickly stop here to let you rest a spell and cool down. I believe we have the time. That ole army dog is most likely still cleaning your nightly offering out of his ears and nose." Watching the cabin to be sure he had not been spotted as he let them drink. It was a good way's off and *it was unlikely any one would notice, but one does have to be careful. Especially when you're on the lam as we are. The sergeant is a little upset with me and horse he just might hang you now with you helping me.* Gray Wolf smiled at the thought of it all. *Hanging a horse, that would be one for the history books.*

Letting them take their time drinking from the stream as he looked around for any movement, Gray Wolf, quietly smiled as he considered the idea of the next trap he would leave for that Pawnee Tracker. *Most likely by now he is not far behind and angry as a whole mess of robbed honey bees. Well, horse, whatever your name is they are going to have to kill me before they get me. I am no planter; I was born free and will die free. No body is going to fence me in on a dried-out riverbed I will hang first. But let me tell you…* "You need a name," Gray Wolf said as he stopped to consider the thought. "Thunder, you have a white line on your face that looks like, maybe lighting. How about Mr. Thunder?" Gray Wolf put his hand under his head and lifted it up and looked him eye to eye as he said, "Yes. I think Mr. Thunder will do." Mr. Thunder seemed to not care other than pulling away to grab a mouthful of grass growing beside the stream.

Gray Wolf let them graze as he eased back over the back trail. No one was in sight as the way was clear for a good hundred yards. Walking back to retrieve Mr. Thunder as he mounted up and checked to be sure the rope holding the pack horse was still secured to the saddle horn, most of the times he did not use a saddle, but the army in their generosity had so provided freely. Might as well be sociable and use them as it does make travel a little easier and gives a horn to tie the pack horse to.

He gently nudged him with his knees through the stream. Walking them upstream away from the cabin a good 50 yards before coming up on the other side. The tracks clearly showed his way out as he laughed. "Just keep on coming Army Dog."

Looking around for a good stand of trees or rocks that could use to conceal himself and protect the horses from the spray of bullets as he considered his next move. Looking up the sun was getting low in the West, only a couple of hours of daylight left. "Mr. Thunder, we could rest up and wait for them to catch up. Have us a little funning at their expense, those troopers need a little excitement now and then to living up their lives. Tracking a harmless ole Kiowa has got to be tiring. I think we should give them something to write home to their ma about. What do you think Mr. Thunder?"

After riding a half hour more, he came across a heavy stand of trees. "Well now, this will do right nicely. You think Mr. Thunder?" he said as he jumped off? Dropping the saddle, then he staked out the horses to allow them to graze as he moved back to the edge of the growth to watch his back trail. No one was in sight, although dust could be seen rising in the distance. About a half mile out, getting close to the stream. "That would be a good place for them to camp. We have a good view of the stream from this upper position," he whispered to himself.

About a half-hour later, they rode up to the stream and stopped to water their horses as they refilled their canteens. Gray Wolf watched as the Sergeant seemed to give orders to set up the camp. Wanting to start his own fire, but it would be too risky until the night had set in as the smoke could be seen rising. After dark, they would not notice the smoke hanging in the air as their own would cover his and as long as he used a few large rocks along with the heavy growth of trees to cover the small fire light he should be okay with his own camp as it was a good half mile out.

Getting everything together, Gray Wolf waited until an hour after sunset to get his own fire going as he made plans of which he had amused himself with. It could not have worked out any better with the location the troopers had chosen to set up camp.

Gray Wolf sipped his coffee and took the time to cook some rock bread from the flour he had relieved from the troopers. Sitting by the fire surrounded by the trees, his little encloser made him feel safe for the moment. Until he heard a voice behind him. "Thought you had me with that rotten horse, huh?"

Gray Wolf quickly stood up with rifle in hand as he faced the Pawnee Tracker. In a panic, he quickly looked around for any troopers, there were none, only the

Pawnee. Smiling, White Hawk walked over to the fire and sat down. "Coffee?"

"Yes, Tracker you can have a cup."

"Kiowa, that rotten horse was a bit over kill."

"Pawnee, it worked. If you were on to it, why did you not turn me in?"

"Not ready to. You see, I want to prove that no Kiowa can break me from his trail. You see Gray Wolf, this is between us, a Pawnee and a Kiowa. We are playing a game, you run, I find."

"How did you know about the horse?"

"I have known of others to have use that same trick, I have used it. Hid inside the stinking hide of a rotten buffalo bull to lose pony soldiers back when we were many."

"Okay, but you did not come and check to see if I was there."

"I did not have to Kiowa. The buzzards gave you away. They all soared up as you dug your way under the carcass."

"Why did you not turn me in?"

"Gray Wolf, the American's have pushed all the tribes out including my own people. Yes, I work for them and track their runaways, but you are making a fool of the Sergeant, which I do not care for. Yes, I follow you as I must, although giving you a chance to get away with the pranks along the way is very rewarding. The stick trap was good, you almost got me with that one. The only reason it didn't was you brushed clean the area around it and you should have tossed over a few leaves, twigs, and grass around it."

"So, what happened, if you did not spring it, who did?"

"The Sergeant's horse stepped on it and tossed horse piles over the whole get-together. You should have seen it, the Sergeant had it from his leg all the way up to his neck and the rest went over and sprinkled like scatter shot over the others." White Hawk said as he laughed.

Gray Wolf was not sure what to make of it as the tracker had him, but did not seem concerned about turning him in. "I do not understand Pawnee, should I kill you, thank you, or run?"

"Gray Wolf, you make fools of the troopers. For now, you are safe, Sergeant Mason thinks you are much further ahead. I think you might reach the mountains if you do not try too many games. But you need to win one for the People-Of-The-Land and I am going to look the other way and let you have your fun. Not long, but long enough for you to get to the foot hills. There I think you will fade into the rocks."

"White Hawk, you can bet your tommy-hawk on it. I know places, paths there that no Trooper or Pawnee can follow."

"I believe that to be true, and look forward to the chance to see. Gray Wolf, you have made it hard to keep up with you as you have used all the tricks I was ever taught. Your games have made this entertaining and I will tell of this around the camp fires to my yet to be born grandchildren. The rope across the path yesterday has slowed the Sergeant hurting his back."

"But why Tracker?"

"Gray Wolf, you have great courage, circling back to walk among the enemy, steal their horses, take their food, and burn their wagons. You are bold with more brass than an army cannon, or missing a few pickles from your clay jar. You have angered the great bear; The Sergeant talks of hanging you now and your life depends on you reaching the mountains. Not that it matters to me if you live or die."

"Tracker, you are a liar as my life does matter to you, I believe the only reason you have not turned me in is the Sergeant. You detest the Sergeant more than enough to let me live long enough to make a complete fool of him. Tracker, you can best believe that Sergeant of yours will remember the name of Gray Wolf, along with his children's children and you telling stores of this around campfires with great laughter. I have not even started to open my bag of tricks."

"I believe that is true, Kiowa, you have great spirit watching over you. We are enemies, with a common enemy, so I guess that makes us friends. We will see who must die. Maybe you will live, maybe not. But when it comes time for us to kill each other, it will be in combat. But for now, I will enjoy watching the Sergeant boil."

"How did you find me tracker?"

"Oh, I asked myself what would I do after I found where your horse relieved himself over by the stream. I knew you were close as it was still warm. You could not be more than 30 minutes out. After walking out a piece and I spotted these trees. Only place around, I knew this was a good place, but the only place you could be. Now Kiowa, come day-light you won't be here as I will have to bring the troopers here and watch them hang you if you are."

"Don't you lose a minute's sleep Tracker, by day light, I will be miles away from here. They are not going to force this old hunter to become a planter. I was born here and will die here; the spirits of my ancestors walk here as mine will as well."

"Sleep well Kiowa, you have my word you are safe until first light. After that you must run or die."

"Tracker, you found me this time; it won't happen again; I will not make it so easy next time as I underestimated you. You're better than I thought, or lucky."

Not another word was said as Gray Wolf watched him put his cup down and walk out into the night and vanish into the darkness. Not sure whether to believe a

Pawnee or not. Gray Wolf decided his best bet was to sleep a couple of hours and get an early start. Traveling at night would be slow, but hopefully there would be a bright moon up later. Bedding down next to the fire as sleep came quickly.

Three hours later, with a full moon sitting high in the early morning sky, the night glowed bright as Gray Wolf finished his second cup of coffee. He quickly estimated that it was around mid-night with seven hours until light. "Well now," he gently whispered to himself with a sly smile. The camp would be asleep and would not expect a visit from an old friend. "If I could find those loco weeds growing that I passed earlier, in the dark I could slow them down."

Laying a few sticks on the fire, he quickly picked up his blanket and a bag with mixed paints made from ashes, berries, and clay he kept with him and eased out into the night. Slowly making his way back toward the stream where the troopers had made their camp. Looking around for the familiar plants that could be easily spotted growing even in the light of the moon. He quickly located them and pulled up several plant using his blanket as a bag to carry them in as he eased his way toward the camp. The light of the fires illuminated the camp with only a single guard on duty sitting on a tree stump drinking coffee. The horses were in a rope corral not far behind the sleeping troopers.

Going upstream to cross, so as not to alert the guard, Gray Wolf held his package of loco weed high above his head as he slowly made his way across the slow-moving water. Careful not to splash or trip on a stream rock which would alert the guard. Easing up onto shore with the water dripping from his now wet body caused him to shiver from the cool night air. Taking a minute to let some of the excess water drip from his wet deer leather shoes and clothes as he held the blanket full of loco weed close to help warm his cold body. After a few minutes, he slowly made his way over the short distance to the rope holding in the horses as he kept a close eye on the guard which seemed to be sleeping with his head down as he sat on a wood box leaned against a tree. Slowly easing his way around to the back of the rope corral, Gray Wolf slowly poured out the loco weed to the horses as he gently whispered, trying hard not to alarm them along with waking up the camp.

Easing back after he had emptied his blanket of midnight snacks for them, he turned his attention to the camp. The Pawnee tracker was nowhere in sight, most likely sleeping in one of the darker areas. *No matter,* the Sergeant was clearly in sight, smiling, Gray Wolf slowly made his way through the camp keeping a close eye on the guard. Occasionally stopping as the guard moved his head as he slept. Glancing over, the horses were nibbling at the generous meal he had provided them. With them eating the loco weed, it would not give him much time he would have to work fast.

The camp was quiet except for the occasional snore, trickling of the stream, and hoot of an owl. After making his way through the maze of troopers sleeping close together, he kneeled next to the sleeping Sergeant. Quietly, he reached into the little leather pouch he had brought along filled with paints he had put together for this occasion. Smiling as he selected each color to gently paint the sergeants face. He gently applied a generous amount as he painted the Sergeant for war. Then as if that was not enough, he took his pistol along with his holster he had laying on his bed roll by his side. Then just as he turned to leave, he spotted the Sergeant's new leather boots. Sitting down as he pulled off one of his wet trail-worn deer leather moccasins; a trade came to mind. Pulling off the other one and sitting them by the sergeant's side, he slowly eased the new boots from the sergeant's side as he checked to be of sure of a good fit. Comparing his foot seemed to indicate a good match. Looking around the troops, most had taken their boots off as they slept. Moving around he collected several pair and quietly laid them in the camp fire. Smiling, as he slowly eased out barefooted holding his new army boots, Gray Wolf eased toward the stream and quietly crossed over before putting on his new boots.

A little loose, but they would work out fine. Although they crunched as he walked. The new leather would have to be broken in. Quickly, Gray Wolf made his way back to camp, having no more than three hours before sunup. Wasting no time, he quickly saddled up and packed up the supply horse and checked their hooves to be sure there were no rocks stuck in them. Remembering the shoes, he had removed earlier, he pulled them out and tossed them over into the fire. Leading the horses out before he jumped on. Reluctantly, the horses galloped out.

"Well supplied with enough food to last a month, a new pair of boots, and enough ammo to hunt through the winter if needed. What more could he ask for?" he whispered as he smiled and looked back toward the direction of the camp of his new found friend. *Friend or enemy, who would believe a Kiowa could be agreeable with a Pawnee. We have a common enemy for now anyway, an enemy that will be in no hurry to break camp.*

CHAPTER THREE

"What the blazes!" Private Thomas screamed as the horses started falling down and shaking their legs in the air. It was his turn to stand guard ,but he could not find his boots as he noticed the horses. Waking the others as they looked around for their boots and some were missing. The Sergeant jumped up and reached for his boots that were not there. He stopped after he saw Private Layton looking intensely at him.

"What are you looking at Private."

"Sir it's your face…"

"Well…What about my face?" the Sergeant asked?

"Well Sir you are painted for war," he replied as the others had now stopped and were also looking.

Reaching for a shaving mirror even in the dim light of the now growing fire he could see the war paint. "The Kiowa is playing games; he is dead when we catch up to him," he said as he reached for a pan of water to wash it off with. "Now find my boots."

"Sir they are gone along with some of the others, look in the fire?"

Looking over, there was burned leather outside of the fire where they had been tossed. It was only after he washed the paint off that he turned his attention back to the horses that were falling down and banging their heads on the tree trunks the rope was tied around.

"Sir it is Loco Weed," Private Thomas said after walking over and finding some outside of the rope corral.

"Well Private, get them fed some grain and fresh water from the stream, it should be worn off in a couple of hours."

"Yes Sir," Private Thomas replied as he stumbled over rocks in his bare feet to help get it done.

"Private, get your horse out and walk him around to the grass over by the stream to clear his head, you need to ride back to the line and get us some boots. You should be back by mid-day sun if you hurry."

"White Hawk, why did you not see this coming?" The Sergeant asked as he watched him walked over to the fire for a cup of coffee.

"Who can tell about that loose in the head Kiowa, Gray Wolf has not done anything normal like get as far away from the troopers as possible, if I were him, I would be miles away from here. Sergeant, he has three times done what is not normal, gone back and robbed the camp, burned your boots, steal your horses, and then try to poison the rest of them. No, that Kiowa is missing a few cards from a full deck. You can never tell what he may do."

"White Hawk, I believe it is more of a game with him, taking chances. No, Gray Wolf is getting past my guards, now that we know this, we will use it and next time we will be ready. Private Thomas, you got them horses about straightened out?" The Sergeant screamed.

"Yes Sir, I think mine is anyway, he is rideable."

"Good, then it is starting to break light, get back to the line and get us some boots and Private, bring back Boomer."

"Boomer Sir? That crazy hound doesn't like me Sir. I can't…"

"Then bring the old man with him, he can tame the hound. Whoever is missing their boots, give Thomas your boot size, and Thomas don't lollygag. This has become personnel between that Kiowa and me. It has gone from taking him back to line now we are going to hang him on sight."

"Yes Sir, Boots and old man Shane with his dog." Thomas replied as he saddled up to leave.

"Now White Hawk, what do you think he will do next?"

"Sergeant nothing, I would have done fits him, I guess everything I would not have done, like ride slow and wait to see what we will do"

"Then he could be just ahead?" The Sergeant asked as he screamed to saddle up to the boys, "boots or no boots we ride in our stockings. We got us a Kiowa to catch, along with getting back our supplies."

He was far out, but he could see them as he watched them break camp and saddle up. Gray Wolf smiled as he watched the troopers complaining of hurting their feet on the saddle stirrup. Even the Sergeant took longer as he pushed himself up into the saddle.

"Well White Hawk?" the Sergeant screamed as he gave the order to move out with White Hawk running out across the stream.

Leading them straight to Gray Wolf's camp site as he slowly looked for sign to give him time to break camp. He was going to help the Kiowa a little, but not much. A half hour later, he walked into his camp with the troopers behind him. It was empty, ashes were cold and something stood out in the cold ashes.

"What's that in the ashes?" Sergeant asked as he looked around. Reaching down and pulling them out. Horse shoes, "well now, he no longer has a limping horse does he White Hawk? Guess we cannot plan to catch him so easy, but how would he have removed them without tools. I guess I should not be so surprised, he took everything else why not shoeing tools. I should not be surprised to find out he has enough tools to build a house, I guess the better question is what did he not take? It seems he has anything needed. He has enough of our supplies to start a business." The sergeant said, as he rubbed his chin in frustration as he watched White Hawk.

White Hawk stood quietly as he considered the now vacant campsite. Why would he have thrown them into the fire, burying them would have seemed the better choice. Unless he wanted us to find them. Then the clear boot prints around the fire are there to antagonize the Sergeant, his boots with Gray Wolf's feet in them. Smiling, he did not point them out to the sergeant. *This Kiowa likes to play games.*

"Sergeant, the ashes are cold, meaning he left well before day break. Gray Wolf is now running to get ahead and make it to the mountains which are still a couple of days ride from here. He wanted you to find the shoes let you know nothing is holding him back now."

"Nothing is going to hold me back either; we will push him until that hound gets here and then we should quickly catch him. Now White Hawk point the way."

Looking around as he turned to leave, White Hawk slowly looked for sign. looking over each print carefully. The sergeant gave him time to get ahead and screamed for the troopers to move out slowly.

They had not gone more than a mile before White Hawk stopped and allowed the troopers to catch up.

"What seems to be the problem White Hawk?" the Sergeant asked as he rode up.

"A shaving glass."

"A shaving glass, Where?"

"Just above your head Sergeant, hanging in the limb." But before White Hawk could warn him, Private

Layton had rode up beside the Sergeant and reached up and pulled it down as a shot rang out and he fell to the ground. The troopers jumping to the ground in panic as they rushed behind rocks. White Hawk only watched as he noticed the mirror shatter into a hundred pieces and scatter across the ground with Layton falling from his horse dead. Shot through the face. Layton had pulled it down to look at it.

The Sergeant never moved as he watched his troops jump behind the rocks. "White Hawk, these boys may not live long enough to become trained in the willy ways of Indian warfare. Green recruits, most all of them, some from Eastern cities. "Boys!" he screamed out, "you are safe now, as long as you do not pick up any of the glass. Private Johnson, you and a couple of the boys tie him to his horse and send it on his way back to camp for burial."

It was about that time, Private Thomas returned leading a pack horse loaded with supplies and a chow wagon in tow.

"Happy to see you," Private Thomas said as he rode up and saluted the Sergeant. "Your trail was at times was hard to follow. Captain Lowe sent this chow wagon back with me' thought we could use a hot meal after I explained to him it may take a while to catch this one."

"That sounds fine Private, a hot meal and you got my boots in that pack?"

"Yes sir, I do,"

"Get your boots out Boys!" the sergeant screamed out.

They wasted no time as they found their right boot size and put them on. "Nice to be back in boots again, from here on out, I am going to sleep in these. That crafty Kiowa ain't a going to get these; now what about my dog Boomer, you were supposed to bring back the hound, well where is he?"

"Sorry Sir, Lieutenant Noland would not allow me to have him, said the captain wanted all of the dogs including Boomer for night duty to help maintain the line. Said there was going to be no more escapes from the line."

"Thomas that hound could have made this job a mite easer, most likely quicker. Sending a chow wagon on this trail will only last a day or two before I have to send it back. That Kiowa is headed to the mountains and it's going to get rough and the trails sometime will not be wide enough for a horse. But even so, I do think a hot meal would be good for the men. But we are moving out, please try to keep up and keep as close to us as you can. But if it should reach a time and it will; that wagon cannot go any further, send him back. We will not wait up."

"Yes sir," Thomas said as he saluted, and watched the sergeant look around to be sure they had their boots on and scream out an order for the troopers to, "mount up and move out!"

White Hawk had not wasted any time as he picked up the trail and was moving fast and then he suddenly came to an abrupt stop.

Catching up to White Hawk, the sergeant waited as he watched him step onto a low rock. White Hawk looked hungerly toward the mountains range in the distance. "Wasting time White Hawk, he is moving as we stand still. He is your enemy and ours. The army pays you to track and we feed you good, do we not? You have an Army issue rifle, good boots to wear, and an army issued blanket to keep you warm at night. You get sick, you have an army doctor to look after you. Blazes, White Hawk, if you die, the army will even supply you with a fine wooden box for burial. True, you are always out on the next trail hunting some army deserter, renegade, or helping in some way. But White Hawk, somehow, this one is different. You seem to be holding back as if you are afraid, or maybe allowing Gray Wolf to pull the wool over your eyes."

"Mountains hold death. Maybe mine, maybe yours. Then maybe Gray Wolf will die. Great Sprits show me vision in night of blood in those mountains. I follow his trail; he does much to cover his tracks, he uses old tricks, creates false trails, and seems to make up a few tricks of his own. Sometimes it is like tracking a shadow which leaves no trace of his passing. I have to circle until I find a broken stick, grass, or a turned stone. Gray Wolf is careful and plans out his steps even for his horses.

Brushing out their tracks when he needs to lose us and then other times, he leaves clear easy to follow tracks when he wants us to follow him. Plays tricks, the mirror, and rope across the trail, he left us clear tracks to follow. No Sergeant, he is like an old mountain lion. He knows all the tricks used by the old ones. He is going to be tough to snag, we will. But it will not be today, tomorrow, or a few days from now. This one will only be caught after he is worn down."

The sergeant sat quietly for a moment, then looked around and called for the troops to mount-back up as some had dismounted. Walking over, he slowly stepped up into the saddle. Sitting quietly, thinking for a moment, he looked down at White Hawk. "I know I have said this before, when we do catch that Kiowa, we will hang him on the spot, I have no plans of doing this again and tying up much needed troops that should be guarding the line. This little game of his has cost Private Layton his life and he will pay for that. If I find out you are helping him by holding back, you will hang with him."

White Hawk did not answer or give any indication of concern as he turned and stepped down from a tree stump, he had stepped up on to get a better view. Slowly leading them out. Behind him, the Sergeant gave the order to move out. The troops quickly formed a line as they moved out with White Hawk now running toward the mountains, he was sure he would pick-up the tracks. Gray Wolf had brushed out making it hard to follow, this only worked for a short distance to help slow anyone following. Truly, White Hawk needed no tracks to keep pace as it was clear Gray Wolf was headed to the mountains as fast as his horse could get him there. Looking for tracks only to appease the Sergeant. True, Gray Wolf was using ever trick he knew to cover his trail. White Hawk had to admit to himself he was, as the Sergeant had said, 'holding back' he could have had Gray Wolf many times. He is using most of the standard ways to try to break his trail. Even tapping, a termed to describe what a coon does to throw off a dog on his trail, going up one tree and crossing over to come down another one. Not that Gray Wolf had climbed a tree, but he would lay down a trail and make it seem to go one way and come out on another trail.

It had taken over an hour before the tracks were located, moving towards the mountains as White Hawk had expected. He had found the tracks along with Gray Wolf's camp site, the ashes of his campfire were warm only hours old, the horse nuggets were moist, and where he had dumped his coffee, the ground had not dried. Gray Wolf had done nothing to conceal where he had camped as he stopped to eat and make coffee. *Is this Kiowa loose in the brain, or is this a game, a game to torment the Sergeant? Could it be that he and the Kiowa have a common enemy? If so, what had the Sergeant done besides follow orders to bring him back in? A conquered people the Kiowa, as were all Indian nations. Why single out the Sergeant or was this a death wish. Is this Kiowa trying to get caught as he had camped not more than a half mile out from them, he could have easily seen the camp fires of the troopers burning as they lit up the night sky?* Then he saw it, the empty shell case on the ground. Why would he have left it here?

"Giving us our bullets back, empty?" The sergeant said as he saw it.

White Hawk did not answer as he moved out. Looking for tracks, for the moment they were deep, easy to follow and it worried him. White Hawk kept pace as the troopers followed close behind. Watching for any tricks Gray Wolf may have in store as White Hawk pushed to catch up to him. Then he came up to a clearing and the tracks vanished. Gray Wolf had swept them out. Walking a few paces forward, White Hawk noticed fresh dirt with leaves and sticks scattered around. But before he could put it all together and could warn the sergeant, his horse stepped into the middle of the area. A sound of swish could be heard and a stick popped up with a nest filled with horse fertilizer being thrown up into the air. The Sergeant's leg was covered with the rest landing on the troopers, a few yards behind him.

One trooper got an eye full. But mostly, it landed on their legs and saddle horns. Except the sergeant, which it covered his left leg. This sent him into a raging fit as he jumped from his horse and kicked dirt into the air.

Throwing out a few choice words and lost his religion before he stopped to realize all eyes were on him.

"White Hawk, did you know that was there?" He calmly asked.

"Wasn't sure until your horse stepped there. I was trying to figure out why he had swept the area clean with fresh dug dirt being covered in leaves and sticks."

"Your ancestral hatred of the Kiowa goes back many generations, you were raised to understand them, kill them, and know their ways. Please try to be a little faster next time," he said as he used a stick to knock off as much he could and emptied his canteen washing it off.

White Hawk moved on and ignored them as they cleaned up, he pushed on and they would have to catch up. he found his tracks, but now they were leading toward the direction of Cripple Creek. *Gray Wolf has shown himself to be a risk taker. But Cripple Creek could be his death, most likely trying to make me believe he is headed there and will hide his trail later as he changes back toward the lower mountain trail. As I was getting ready to push hard to try to catch up to him, I heard the chow wagon coming up with pans rattling, barrels rocking, and the cook screaming at the team of mules as they were about to run down a couple of troopers in their way.* That biscuit and ham I had earlier was gone, and a cup of coffee would be good here past high noon. *Gray Wolf could wait, and I'm sure it would not bother him if his trail gets a couple of hours cold as we let the horses and men take a break.* Walking back as I watched the troops stake out their mounts. The cook jumped off and tossed out some wood he had collected earlier with hot coals he was carrying in a pig iron pot. It helped to speed the process up as he kept the coals from his last fire closed up in the pot, he carried around hanging off the back of the wagon. In no more than 10 minutes, he had the coffee on, beans heating up and a slab of beef roasting away. The smell carried by the wind was sure to reach Gray Wolf which could only enjoy his tormented taste buds as we enjoyed the moment.

CHAPTER FOUR

"That fool is headed toward Cripple Creek," the sergeant said as he watched White Hawk change direction. "He is headed there to spend my boot money. We'll corner the rat there," he said as he rode past White Hawk.

"Sergeant, you are stepping on the tracks!" White Hawk screamed as he rode by. "

White Hawk, there is no need to track now, he is headed to the watering hole with my boot money."

"Sergeant, it will be dark in an hour, not much you can do we need to be setting up camp."

Knowing that White Hawk was right, the Sergeant reined to a stop and ordered his men to set up camp. The mess wagon was behind them and traveled slow and would not be caught up for a good half hour. Unsaddling the horses and staking them out to graze gave it time to catch up.

"About blasted time you got here!" the sergeant screamed as Deeds pulled in.

Metal pans rattling, and wheels screaking for want of hub grease. "Sorry Sergeant, I had me a mess of trouble back aways and had to stop. Awheel was wobbling and the hub nut was about to come off. Had to stop and push the wheel back on and tighten the hub nut. Hard to do by your lonesome and all the weight still on the wheel."

"Well, no harm done, get the coffee on and some vittles fired up, the boys are hungry and I could use a plate full myself."

"Yes sir, Sergeant," he responded as he saluted and walked away to get the fire going.

"White Hawk, how far you reckon we are from Cripple Creek? Can we be there first light? I want to get there before he has time to sober up and be out of town."

"Sergeant, I believe we could be there a couple of hours after sun-up. If we got an early start."

"Early start, I'll have these boys up and, and in the saddle, long before first light. You hear that boy's, bed down as soon as you finish chow."

Walking out into the now twilight as he watched the last rays of the sun die out over the horizon. White Hawk, looked out into the distance, "you may have done it this time Kiowa." He whispered to himself. "Hope you are smart enough to not overdo it, or he will have you nailed to a stake this time." Standing outside of camp until the sun rays disappeared over the horizon. Only then did he return back to the chow wagon to get some coffee and beans with boiled ham.

Waking up hours before dawn as he looked around, everyone slept soundly except for the two on guard duty. They moved around knowing better than to fall asleep after the scolding the sergeant had given them after Gray Wolf had raided the camp, not twice, but three times now. Losing his boots, painting his face for war, and scattering the horses with live ammunition in the campfire had the sergeant in a raging anger.

It is common knowledge that the troopers keep a few coins in their boots, but that Kiowa must have hit the bank to be headed to town by the way the sergeant was acting.

Not allowing time for a cup of coffee. Giving orders to saddle up right out of the bed roll. The chow wagon would have to follow and maybe in a few hours, he can set up just outside of Cripple Creek and the men could eat if the sergeant managed to head off Gray Wolf there.

"White Hawk, catch us at Cripple Creek!" the Sergeant screamed as he rode out.

With that order Gray Wolf jumped onto the chow wagon and rode with the wagon master for the next two hours and he had never seen such a rough way to go. That wagon hit every bump, his ears went numb from Deeds screaming at the mules pulling it, and his back ached from the hard wood seat. If he could have kept up, he would have walked.

"White Hawk, how do you figure it? That Kiowa going to town"" Deeds asked. "You would think that would be the last place he would go."

"No Wagon Master, it is not, he was raised around white men, his sister is married to one. He can and knows the language well, knows the ways of a town. I have heard he has a great taste for beer and will think nothing of walking into a saloon. He has got into trouble when he was refused service. Down Texas way, I am told he tore apart a Mexican Cantina, killed a man over a glass of beer, and has escaped hanging twice. But I don't believe any of that to be true. Gray Wolf seems to have caused a lot of campfire tales to grow each time they are told."

"Yes, I see what you mean, I know a few men like that. Read about them anyway."

"You're a reader Wagon Master?" White Hawk asked as he picked up a copy of Old West magazine off of the floorboard? "Never have learned to read myself, I am told the Kiowa can a little. White men have a word for everything. Strange shapes on paper mean things. Do you read Wagon Master?"

"Yes, I do. My ma taught me to read and write, do a little arithmetic as well."

"What does this say here?" What Hawk asked as he pointed to the front cover?

"Scatter Gun Roy, Stagecoach Driver has been stopped a dozen times with attempted holdups. None have managed to rob him or any of his passengers. Most have met their fate at the end of his barrel, a 10-gauge scattergun ended any who tried. Few got away, with a sizable lot others meeting their fate on boot hill."

"Their fate, what does that mean?"

"It means he killed them and they were buried in the outlaw cemetery If there was enough to bury. A 10-gage scattergun can put a sizable hole in a man. Make bird feed out of you."

"It really says all of that Wagon Master?"

"It does on the next page. I have read it so many times I know it by heart."

"This Scatter Gun Stage Coach Driver, where does he hail from?"

"New Mexico Territory, least ways that is what the paper says. Could be altogether someplace else. They write whatever sales as most of these are about outlaws, but sometimes they do stories of lawmen and in this case a stagecoach driver from New Mexico Territory. According to the story his coach is always full as riders pay extra to be on his stage as they feel safer or did. He died, shot with his own gun by his dog bumping it over. He went everywhere with him, Ole Smoky, his trusted hound. I suppose most of the story is just that a story. Those writers will write just about anything to sell their magazines. I am sure telling it a little taller to help the numbers would not be a problem for them."

"I don't know Wagon Master, being shot by your own dog, I just don't know. I have known a couple that was shot by their wives. Black Bear was shot by his own, caught him in another's wigwam."

"You sound like a man of great knowledge to females Mr. Hawk." "Oh no, I have never taken one. No one to direct my trails. I go and come as I see fit."

"Getting light, our conversation has allowed the time to flow by Mr. Hawk, it is breaking day and the town is just ahead. I think I will let you take it from here and I shall wait here and see what the Sergeant finds. It could be we have reached the end of our journey and can return back to the line."

"Wagon Master, if I know Gray Wolf, our journey has only started. He will not allow himself to be…"

"What is it Mr. Hawk?" Deeds asked as he glanced around to see what had suddenly caught his attention.

"Oh, nothing Wagon Master." White Hawk said as he spotted Gray Wolf slowly riding out. Looking around, he saw no one else and more important not the sergeant.

"You know Wagon Master, I think I will wait here with you. Do you think the sergeant would mind if you made some coffee as we wait?"

"Mr. Hawk, I can't think of any reason he would; the men will be hungry and I am sure they would like something to eat." Deeds said as he climbed down and headed to the back to get a fire started.

Watching the wagon master jump down. White Hawk stepped around to the other side of the wagon and looked around for the sergeant. He was nowhere in sight. Turning as he watched Gray Wolf ride out of sight, slowly riding as if he had no care in the world. White Hawk could not help but smile as he considered the brass that Kiowa had, the sergeant would hang him and he rides out like it is of no concern. Shaking his head as he walked around to the back of the wagon and watched Deeds get the fire going.

"White Hawk, do you think the sergeant might need you? If he finds that Kiowa, he could want you to…"

"No Wagon Master, he will send one of the boys back if he should need me. I don't feel like he is going to find him here, most likely he is long gone. I would say about day light." Walking back around the wagon and looking down the street, he could see the sergeant and his troopers coming back and he did not look a bit too happy. Leaning against the wagon as he waited.

"Missed him, and no one saw him leave." The sergeant complained as he walked up. "That Kiowa is giving me an early grave."

"Coffee will be ready shortly," Deeds called out. "You want me to put on some eggs Sergeant?"

"No Wagon Master, coffee is enough. Me and the boys are going over to have a steak after we down a cup of your coffee. Might as well enjoy a little town hospitality as we are here."

"You sure Sergeant?" a private asked?

"Yes, a steak. only no beer, liquor, or girls. We are going to be pulling out of here in a couple of hours and get back on that dog's trail. I want that Kiowa and he has already out-lasted me by days. He has made a total liar of me, I said he would already be in chains, hung, or tied to the back of the wagon. After that little trick with our boots, he tossed into our campfire and loco weeding the horses. That cost us a half a day getting their heads clear. White Hawk, what do you think his next move is?"

"Maybe he will ride hard and fast as he has to know you are close on his trail. Question is, which end of town did he leave from, if he was even here? Oh, he was here alright the stable master said that. But he thinks he left about two hours before sunup. Has no idea which way he went. But I have got to give these boys a breather to eat something besides beans and bacon. A steak should get them back going. You ready Boys?" the sergeant said as he sat down his cup and headed toward town with them following.

CHAPTER FIVE

After having rode until sunup, Gray Wolf felt it was safe enough to stop for a quick meal and let the horses rest a little while. Staking them out to graze as he started a quick fire for coffee. Which it did not take long with a lot of dry branches lying about and dry grass for a starter material. Quickly setting them up. Gray Wolf, pulled a few quick strikes on his flint rock and a glowing spark landed getting the job done. Blowing on it and it gently came to life. As the fire slowly grew, Gray Wolf nervously looked around paying great attention to his back trail. That Pawnee had proven to be every bit the tracker he was. Walking around, he noticed the right boot hurt his foot. It seemed to be the right size, but something kept rubbing his ankle. Sitting down, he pulled off the boot which seem to have something stuck in it. Reaching in, he noticed a cut in the boot liner. Something seem to be pushed into it. Reaching in, he pulled out two paper $10 Dollar bills and a $20 gold piece.

"Well now Sergeant, you old pack rat, squirreling a little something away for a rainy day, you were thinking about this thirsty old Kiowa, I had thought about swinging by Cripple Creek, but now I have good reason too. Enjoy a beer before heading up in those hills. He whispered to no one. Putting his boot back on as he smiled at the thought of having $40.00 and a night on the town. They had rules about Indians in town, but he was no broke Indian. Money only comes in one color and that is spendable. No store keeper will turn away a gold $20, not from anyone that is ready to turn loose of it.

Getting the coffee on as the sun rose high in brought chills along with it as the wind picked up. Pulling up his jacked as he sat back and ate some dry deer jerky he found in his supplies. Waiting for the coffee to get ready. There was no way that Pawnee could show up here as they had to be miles back, if up and going at all. Not having horses or boots would have caused the sergeant to send back to the line to get more, costing him a couple of days easy. The horses will be alright after a few hours, but most likely he wouldn't wait. *This should give me time for a couple of days to enjoy my new found wealth. My good fortune, mighty thankful Sergeant that you stashed up three months pay.* Laughing as he considered it.

Pouring a cup of coffee as he thought about what he could do with that much money. *A night on the town, some mighty good vittles and a couple of bottles to go. My bones could get mighty cold up there. Yes, I will need a couple of bottles of liquid sunshine to brighten my day.*

After drinking a couple of cups, he was in a hurry to get going. Quickly packing up his few supplies he had taken out, he hit the trail leading straight to Cripple Creek. It was then, as he packed up. a mirror fell out of the pack. *Well now this thing might come in handy* he said as he placed it in his coat pocket. He was about to pull out as he spotted White Hawk a way's out.

"Well now you old Army Dog, I'll slow you down," he said to no one as he pulled out the mirror. Riding back a hundred yards as he looked around, he found a branch hanging over the middle of the trail. Stepping up onto the back of his horse to reach it as he tied it up with a leather string. Rushing out to find a higher spot to wait and watch the mirror, he found it a couple of hundred yards out. A large bolder he could hide the horses behind and sit on it and wait. He did not have to wait long as he saw the mirror reflection and shot at it and jumped down. He pushed hard the rest of the day, stopping only to water the horses a couple of times.

Reaching Cripple Creek, as the sun was sinking low, his mounts tired and so was he. Riding up to the stable as the stable master met him at the door. Gray Wolf had on an army coat he had pulled from the supply wagon, army boots, wearing an army issue holster with two army brandied mounts gave the stable master the idea he was a tracker. Gray Wolf left it no other way.

"Can I help you, Tracker?"

"Sure, can Stable Master, my horses have not been cared for all day, they need feed, a good rub down, and a dry stable to rest with plenty of hay."

"Good as done Tracker. What might your name be?"

"Gray Wolf is all I have ever been called."

"Well, mighty pleased to meet you Mr. Wolf. Hope you find our little settlement to your pleasing."

"You have a local watering hole; my gullet is cactus dry?"

"The saloon is right down the street, but understand, the proprietor is a might ornery, the old buzzard is as cantankerous as an old jack ass."

"I'll keep that in mind. Could you drop my supplies and saddles inside their stall?"

"Glad too, be there when you are ready to leave. Mr. Wolf, a word of caution, they have a drink they like to get the greenhorns with, you best leave it alone as it has gun powder, double rum corn squeezing, and a few other things I am not sure about. They call it the, 'Mine blaster'."

"Mine blaster?"

"Yes, this is a mining town and the miners came up with it as a joke on some tinder foot years back, and the saloon keeper, kept using it. The sheriff has asked him not to use it, but he will mind no one. So, stay away from anything that does not come from a bottle."

"Obliged, to you for that, but I can hold my own. Gun powder or not." Walking out, Gray Wolf laughed as he thought of the idea of putting gun powder in a drink. Looking around as he stepped out of the door. The saloon was four building to the right across from the street from the bath house. "Might need to consider going there later, "he whispered to himself as he made a bee line for the Honey Hole Saloon.

Stepping in, it seemed larger on the inside with a small empty stage for Can-Can dancers, a long bar with a few miners and a couple of saloon girls standing around, and several empty tables. Letting go of the swinging doors as he stopped at the entrance to look around. The sound of the doors swinging shut filled the quite room as all talked stopped as Gray Wolf walked in. A large sign hung above the bar, *'No Indians Allowed'*. Ignoring the sign as well as the quite room, Gray Wolf walked up to the bar and dropped the $20.00 Gold piece down. "A beer please?" he asked.

"Indian, can you read? The sign says no Indians allowed."

"Oh, is that what it says, what does that have to do with me? I would like a beer please."

"Well, you're an Indian, are you not? We do not serve Indians here; the owner has those rules."

Gray Wolf stood quite for a minute, "if I were an Indian, I could see that; I met one once, he was a nice enough guy. I would have served him a beer. Now if you do not get me a beer over here, I am going to scap you, right here with these gentlemen here as my witness."

Reluctantly, the bar- keeper relented and poured him a beer. Sitting it down as two miners stepped up beside him. "New to these parts, Mister?" One of them asked as he winked at the bartender.

"No, I have been here before. Last time I was here, some miner offered me a drink called the Mine blaster. You not thinking of getting me to fall for that one again. 'Cause if you are, I just might shoot you. It took me a week to get my head cleared after that one."

"Oh no, we would not do that", they said as they stepped back and headed out the door.

"Bar-keeper, this place is quite as boot hill, where is everyone?"

"Wednesday's church meeting, they're at the evening meeting. They will start flowing in about an hour or so. Where you from, Mister?"

"A lot of places, now leave me alone. I want to enjoy my beer in piece," Gray Wolf said as he downed the last swallow. He pushed the glass out for a refill, which the bar-keeper quickly obliged him and dropped his change down. Picking up his beer, and change as he walking back to the far back table, Gray Wolf sat quietly for the next hour and half, sipping one beer after another. By the time the crowd came in, Gray Wolf was well past one too many. Much to the delight of the miners, Gray Wolf was in no mood to be bothered.

Most of the miners were content to leave him alone. Most, but not Carl. Carl, was always looking to prove something. Weighing 90 pounds dripping wet, 5 foot and missing four front teeth. He was forever trying to prove he was the better man whether it was down in the mine with a pick ax or in the saloon. Which is where he lost his teeth. A cowboy in from a cattle drive came in to rest and enjoy a few beers. Carl had a few shots of Cactus Rose and was ready to take on the world. He made the mistake of crossing the cowboy, stepped on his toe. When he pushed him off, Carl tossed his beer at him. A few punches later and Carl was wrapped up in the corner with his teeth laying on the floor beside him and even then, he did not quit.

Seeing Gray Wolf in his state of well-oiled and in no mood to be bothered inspired Carl to try his luck pestering the old tracker. "Well, what do we have here?" Carl asked sarcastically. "Letting any stray dog in to drink with us hard working miners. Indian, this is our watering hole and we just don't take kindly to just anything slithering in to bellow up."

"Carl, leave him alone," one of the miners responded, "he ain't a harming anyone."

"He's filthy and he smelling up the whole place."

"Carl, you could use a bath yourself," Tinker an old mind blaster said as he walked by. "You are going to lose the rest of your teeth if you don't sit down and leave the old tracker alone."

"Listen here Miner, I only want to relax and have a few beers. I mean no harm. I am about finished and will be leaving in a few minutes."

"No! You will be leaving now Indian." Carl said as he leaned over Gray Wolf pointing his finger in his face. Crowding Gray Wolf is never a good idea, as he back-handed Carl, knocking him to the floor. The room went quiet as the crowd stepped back to allow room for what was coming next. Carl is small, but years of swinging a pickaxe to break open a rock laden load of silver had hardened his small frame of a body. Gray Wolf had no doubts about the fight he had just picked. This little buckshot of a miner had a lot of vented-up frustration from being locked up in a hole far too long. But Gray Wolf had a little steam to blow off as well.

Carl eased up from the floor wiping the blood from his busted lip. "Now Tracker, you have opened up a whole mess of trouble, nobody has ever done that to me and walked away. By the time I am finished with you Indian, you're going to need someone to jaw your food."

Gray Wolf pushed his chair back. "Okay, you little runt, let's see what you have. You have just opened a whole mess of trouble for yourself. You're about to lose a few more of those charcoal black things you call teeth. I haven't whipped me no miner and I can cross that one off my list when I finish here."

Hesitating as he stood up, Carl had not realized how tall Gray Wolf was as he was sitting down. Sizing his up as he rubbed his face to quiet the stinging from the blow. A foot taller and fifty pounds heavier, *this tree might take a little longer to chop down* Carl thought. Leaning down as he went for Gray Wolf's legs. A mistake as Gray Wolf had assumed as much and moved over. This tossed Carl off balance as he rushed in and missed. Gray Wolf kicked him into the wall just behind him as he fell forward bumping his head and falling to the floor. Back on the floor again, Carl went into a mad rage as he kicked a chair out of his way, much to the now gathering crowds and with people stepping into the saloon to see what all the ruckus was about.

"Army dog, you just messed up," he said as he rubbed the knot on his head from hitting the wall.

"Listen Miner, this can stop here, I have no quarrel with you. But if you keep it up, that knot on your head is only going to grow larger."

"I'll knot you Indian, I am going to break you up," Carl responded as he kicked a table out of the way as he rushed up from the floor. Now in a blind rage, he ran head long into Gray Wolf, catching him midsection. Knocking the breath out of him. It took a minute for Gray Wolf to regain himself and this gave Carl enough time to step up onto a chair and lay a hard blow to the side of Gray Wolf's face causing him to fall back. Jumping from the chair, Carl wasted no time as he jumped up onto Gray Wolf's back and locked his legs around his waist and grabbed hold of his shirt collar. All the time smashing hard blows to his head with his free hand.

"Indian, you had enough yet?" Carl screamed in his left ear.

Gray Wolf had had enough of this half-witted mine-rat. Rushing backwards into the corner of the bar, Gray Wolf pushed the miner back against its sharp corner which caused him to scream out in pain. The hold Carl had him loosened as he dropped to the floor in agony screaming his back was broken. "Could be you little nauseating turd," Gray Wolf said with a smile. "Next time you will think before attacking someone, if you ever walk again."

The crowd that had gathered did not hinder Gray Wolf as he picked up his hat and walked out the door. Glancing back as he pushed the swinging doors open, he could see Carl laying on the floor, rolling in pain with no one offing to help him.

"Tracker, you just might have done us a good turn here, this is just about every other night with him," a tall red headed saloon girl said with a wide grin. "Looks like the mine is going to be one man short for a few days, I bet next time the little varmint will think twice before attacking someone. Now maybe things can be a little quieter here, you would think losing his teeth would have been enough."

Gray Wolf did not respond, only walked out slowly as he headed over to a horse trough to lean over and wash the blood from his face. Sitting down on the side of the wood trough, he wiped the water away with his shirt sleeve and rested a minute as he watched four miners pass by carrying Carl as he screamed out in pain holding his back.

"Well Carl, I came here for a little excitement, you sure supplied it." Gray Wolf whispered to himself. "Too bad you were not man enough to take what you dished out. It seems to me you should be man enough to take it if you a going to start it."

"Tracker, you and I could share a bottle and talk about lost loves, long trails, and what great friends we are going to be."

"Good friends and just who are you?" Gray Wolf asked as he looked up to see the town drunk pandering for a drink.

"My name is Sam, most folks here abouts just call me Smokey."

"Well Smokey, that will have to wait as I am going to find a place to bed down and hit the trail come sun-up."

Without saying another word, Gray Wolf quietly moved across the street over to the stable to bed down with his horse in his stall. The warm hay will be a welcome change to the cold hard ground. Walking into the stable which was barely lit with a couple of lanterns turned down low as it made it hard to see. Stumbling his way over he found his horse in a back stall. Pulling up a pile of hay close to his saddle, he fell asleep before his head hit his saddle blanket.

The night went by fast as he was awakened by the sounds of men talking, and he could see the morning sun light coming up through the stable opening lighting up the formally dark building.

He could hear the formular voice of the sergeant. "He has to be here somewhere;" he could hear him say as he peaked around the stable corner. In confusion as he considered how they could have made it to town so fast. *How? They had to send back for boots and let their horses regain their senses.* He had no time to consider the change of events as he quickly and quietly tossed the saddle on his horse and packed up his supplies.

"Well Tracker," he could hear the stable master call out, "you owe me two dollars and you best be busting out of here fast as they are looking for you. I sent them over to boarding house. That should give you a little time to get a jump on them."

Pulling his horses out as he tossed the stable master three silver dollars. "One question I have Stable Master."

"You want to know why I helped you, huh Tracker? Well, you came in here late thirty yesterday evening like you were just plain tuckered out. You headed over to the saloon to have a few quiet drinks and came back over and quietly went to sleep. But I have never seen anyone get the best of that little mine pest, Carl, and besides that. Well, I have you figured as a renegade, you left the line as you were being pushed like cattle to a land you do not want to go to. My grandmother was Kiowa. You're Kiowa are you not?"

"Yes, I am, I will die before they make me beg for blankets, grain, seed, and force me to dig land nobody wants. I am told the land is dry and the hunting is bad. This is the land of my fathers, they died here, I will die here. So far, I have been easy about it all, but if they keep pushing me, I will give them a fight. I will go now and hope that I can get out of town without being seen and if not, I will die here. But so will a lot of them."

"Go in peace, Tracker."

"Thanks, Stable Master," he said as he slowly walked out leading his mount and his pack horse tied to the saddle horn. Easing out the wide stable door, he looked around to be sure he was not seen. Mounting up as he cleared the stable door. He gently nudged his mount forward as he nervously looked back. Only the towns people moved around as they handled their morning business. Slowly, he rode as not to attract attention. After only a few minutes. which had seemed far longer, he made it out. Looking back. everything looked quite enough, the town seemed normal with the wagons moving around bringing in supplies, chickens running around, he could hear the school bell ringing, calling the kids in for their daily studies, passing a wagon loaded with firewood most likely headed to the town diner to supply their wood burning stoves, and a stage coach could be seen coming in from the distance as a trail of dust was pushed up behind it.

Kicking his mount to speed him up, he breathed a sigh of relief as it seemed he had cleared, yet again, he had beat them; could he really think his luck would hold. *Sooner or later, they will catch me, but not today.* Smiling as he looked back and saw no one following him out.

The old sergeant was too slow and his boys too green, but White Hawk was another story. That wily old tracker would be a little harder to fool. Most likely by now, he had figured out that he had slipped out of town and would be hot on his trail again. But maybe, by going back out the way he had come in would be enough to fool him into going the wrong way. Heading out toward the other end of town does make more sense as it is a closer route to the mountains. If he did, he could gain a few hours on him.

The sergeant tried in vain to locate his trail by asking around if anyone had seen a rider leading a pack horse. A miner standing by responded by answering, "Sergeant this is a mining town, there must be dozens of people doing the same thing, who would even notice that as it is done here every day here."

After riding out a couple of miles, Gray Wolf turned and headed back toward the direction he was headed to start with. The mountains loomed ahead, Dead-Man's Pass. That old oak tree stump remains is where he would give them all the slip and if it worked out right, within a couple of days he would be camping there.

Gray Wolf rode steady for the next five hours riding hard until his mount began to lather around his neck and he knew it was time to let them rest, get a drink of water and eat a little fresh grass. Finding a small pool of water with green grass growing around it. He jumped off and let them loose to graze. Looking around he saw he was at the edge of a wide valley. The mountains were just ahead. But already he was gaining sky.

The sun was at midday, straight overhead. Most likely the sergeant was not far behind having discovered he had left as they came in. *Let him come, when I reach those mountains there is rocks a plenty to protect me from any bullets. If they should catch up, I will give them a fight they won't soon forget. Now look at me talking to myself, been out alone to-long.* Laughing as he wiped the sweat rolling down his brow. Looking at his back trail, there was no one to be seen. Miles of nothing but trees, grass, and beautiful land, beautiful green land. Land for everyone, *why do we have to leave the home of our ancestors? There is more than enough for the people, and the planters.*

Sitting down on the ground, he leaned back and closed his eyes to rest a moment. There was the sound of water flowing as he looked around. There was a waterfall, a beautiful waterfall and his mother was standing over on the side of a pool of water looking at him without saying a word. Reaching out as he tried to grab her hand, she only smiled as she turned to walk away.

Opening his eyes, it had only been a dream. But he had slept the afternoon away as the sun was laying low in the west sinking low past the distant mountains. The horses looked up from grazing as he stood up to set up camp and hope those who follow were not close behind as he had slept the past four hours with the mountains blocking the sun rays bringing a quick end to the day. The rest could only mean he had given those who follow time to catch up. White Hawk would not be fooled, he was close. Walking around he could see what looked like faint smoke rising in the distance. Not more than a mile out, if it is them, they are getting close.

"Mister Thunder, how about you and me taking a ride back to see? I will get a small fire going, have my coffee and a little beans and wait for the moon to come up and we will pay them a visit. No tricks tonight, they will look for that okay Thunder? That Pawnee seems to have a little Kiowa in him most likely on his mother's side. Don't you think Thunder?"

"No Kiowa, White Hawk only Pawnee," White Hawk said as he stepped in from the shadows of a large rock he had been hiding behind. Jumping up, White Hawk grabbed his rifle. "You are safe… for now Kiowa." White Hawk said as he smiled. "I have not come to kill you just yet, but you grow lazy. Why you do not hide your tracks, you let me catch up, and taking time to get a beer. You play games? You want to die, the sergeant will kill you, he almost had you back there in Cripple Creek. I had you, watched you ride out."

"Then why did you let me go Pawnee?"

"The war, Kiowa, this is not the first time we have crossed trails. You were captured then and held for a few days. You were younger, but I served under the Greys. They held you for a few days to be sure you were not a spy. Maybe I should have killed you then, a Kiowa."

"Oh, when I am ready, you will die Kiowa, the sergeant will hang you or I will grow tired of this game and shoot you myself. I guess I should kill you and leave your carcass for the birds, hold you for the sergeant, or take you back to camp. But Kiowa, I am enjoying this game, but soon I will tire of this and I do hope you enjoyed your town visit, it will be your last for a long time, maybe forever. Now beer cost money, stables cost money, and you have none. You had no gold until you stole the sergeant's boots and found his squirreled away gold sawbacks he had for a rainy-day. Well, that is what he called it anyway. Now that you have spent it and filled that lake of thirst in your belly, maybe we can get down to some tracking here. Kiowa, I need the challenge and you are going to give it to me or you will die. You see you are supposed to be one of the best 'Smoke' they call you."

"Pawnee after today, you will never get close enough to see my trail dust. Been funning with you, I will admit you are better than I thought, I would have thought that you would have lost my trail sometime back, but yet here you are. Where did you learn to follow a thin trail? I have left little sign, turned rocks in creek water, broken blades of grass, or a broken twig here and there. Enough to rid myself of most trackers. But you hold on like a starving badger to a quail egg. Can't figure you out Pawnee, what is it to you if I live or die? Twice you have caught me and twice you have let me go."

"Let you go? Who says I am going to let you go this time? Maybe I will kill you here myself. Then maybe I like this game of you making a fool of the pony soldiers, stealing their boots, feeding their horses loco weed, and driving the sergeant mad. Yes, I am going to let you go… this time. But don't try to come back to the camp tonight or I will kill you."

"Don't you worry about that Pawnee; I have everything I need now. These fancy army boots, supplies, and two fine horses. I will get me a few hours of sleep and hit the trail headed to leaning rock."

"Leaning rock, no, you are headed to the high mountains to get lost. I know this as that is what I would do. There are many places to hide there, deep caves, hidden valleys, and heavy mountain forest. I am told you know it well, by the women back on the line. They tell stories of you hunting there. You will never catch Gray Wolf; he will vanish and become part of the mountains, like smoke in the rain, or you will take on wings and fly with the soring eagles. Gray Wolf, if you take on wings that I would like to see."

"Females… they talk too much. Pawnee, maybe I will kill you and throw you over the side of flaming rock. There you will wander, lost in the eternal flames and pitch bogs. Your soul tormented by wendigo's that are said to live there. Then I would not have anything else to worry me as the troopers would be easy to lose. Now tell me Pawnee, why should I let you live?"

"Kiowa, if you have not noticed, I am holding the gun and you are sitting down. I can simply shoot you and leave you to the fire. Place enough wood on it to turn you into a roasted duck. No Kiowa, you need me to finish this game or the whole army will be on you with a dozen more trackers, which won't like you as much as I do, giving you a little space. No, I am not worried about you. You need me and in a strange way, I do you. You are my payback to the sergeant as I am enjoying seeing him tormented with your peculiar humor. He still complains about his back from that rope across the trail, you have or had his months' pay, and seeing him covered in horse nuggets was good. Kiowa, as much as I have enjoyed our little talk, I need to get back to camp."

"Don't let me hold you up," Gray Wolf responded as he turned to refill his cup. "But I can tell you… looking up, White Hawk was gone, disappeared back into the night. Leaning back, Gray Wolf closed his eyes and quickly fell asleep being tired from a long day.

Hours later, he was awakened to the sound of his horses nickering. The fire had burned down with only a few hot coal glowing, a quarter moon brightly lighting up the night sky and stars shining brightly, and not a sound from the crickets which spooked him. The horses' heads went up as they looked around. Quickly standing up as he grabbed his rifle and moved behind a large tree to disappear into the dark shadows of the night. He quietly waited to see what had spooked the horses. To his surprise a racoon moved about looking for its nightly meal. Gray Wolf reached into his pocket and tossed it a piece of jerky which it quickly grabbed and disappeared into the night.

After waiting a few more minutes to be sure there was nothing else, Gray Wolf gathered up an arm load of sticks and tossed them onto the glowing embers. It did not take long before the fire was glowing bright and he had a pot of fresh coffee on and sat down with a large piece of deer jerky and waited for the coffee to get ready. He estimated it was three or four hours before sunup and an early start would help get him ahead of those that followed. That would be the smart thing to do, but he never was one to follow the rules. Smiling as he considered vising the troopers camp as it crossed his mind. He had time; they would not be up for a couple of hours. Then he remembered that he had seen a large bag of salt on the chow wagon.

Within the next half hour, he had down a couple of cups of coffee and a handful of deer jerky. Easing out in to the night as he heading in the direction, he assumed the camp to be, it was not long before he spotted a campfire glowing in the distance. Slowly making his way over as he looked around for any guards on duty. There was a couple which both had their head down as they sat on a blanket around the fire. Slowly, he made his way over to the chow wagon and found the salt along with a five-pound bag of coffee which he took as well. Slowly making his way over to the 40-gallon water barrels, he dumped half of the ten-pound bag of salt in each one. Smiling as he replaced the lid. It would not slow them down as they could replace the water quickly. But it would let them know he had been here, taking the coffee would do more to aggravate them.

Slowing looking around, he considered their boots, but decided against it as he was running out of time. Then just as he was about to move out of their camp it hit him. Slowly, he made his way over to the horses and unhobbled each one and removing the rope around them which had made a makeshift corral. slowly he moved back over to the chow wagon and found a box of 45 shells. He tossed them into the fire as he ran out into the night. After he had ran not more than a half dozen steps, he could hear the shots going off and the horses busting free. Someone screaming orders most likely the sergeant as he made his way back to his own camp.

Sunrise found him a mile out and moving fast to put some distance behind him and that blasted Pawnee. The sergeant would hang him for sure now, if he could catch him and the pressure was on the Pawnee to find him, there would be no more of letting him go. But it should have bought him enough time to gain a few miles before they could regroup and round-up the horses. Headed for any point he could make it to that took him to the mountains.

Riding hard and fast over the next couple of hours had pushed his horse to the point of exhaustion as he was lathered over and breathing heavy. Stopping at a small stream of water to let them rest and allow him time to cool down and eat a little deer jerky. The horses took several minutes drinking from the stream before they moved over to the grass growing beside the stream.

Giving them time to rest as he looked around; this would be a good place to come back and spend a few days hunting or fishing. There was sure sign of animal tracks around the stream and fish moved in the stream, but that would have to wait for another time. That

Pawnee was most likely right behind him and Gray Wolf had no doubt that he meant what he said. After a good half hour, Gray Wolf moved the saddle over to the pack horse to let Mister Thunder have a break and carry the lighter load of the pack. He did not wish to lose either one out here.

But before he was able to mount up, he heard a movement behind him. "Don't move Indian," a voice said with authority. Slowly turning around as he looked down the barrel of a Colt cap and ball 44, referred to as the Sunday pistol. The guns were slow to reload, but could blow an arm off or put a hole in a man the size of a Goose Plum. Looking up, it was a ragged dressed army deserter most likely.

"What do you want?" Gray Wolf asked.

"The horses Indian, so step back and we won't have any trouble."

"Army deserter?" Gray Wolf asked? "What are you doing out this way with no horse?"

"That would be none of your affair, I want the horses, their army anyway, stolen most likely. You can steal more and live."

"You sure about that deserter, you see I have a whole heap of you Army boys on my trail, following those two horses. They want me more than you, maybe we could work something out and help each other?"

"The only thing you're going to do Indian, is move away from them horses and hand me that bag." He said as he turned to point at the bag of jerky sitting beside of a rock. That was the last thing he ever said as Gray Wolf pulled his knife from the sheath hanging on his side and threw it into his throat. He was dead before he hit the ground.

"Wrong man, wrong day, Solder boy," Gray Wolf said as he pulled out his knife and wiped the blood from it on the dead man shirt. Turning him over as he pulled off the gun belt and picking up the Colt." Not much of a gun, but it is a gun and will come in handy later," he said as he looked it over. "Not even loaded, you're going to try to rob me with an unloaded gun, Boy, you are crazy and now you are dead. An unloaded gun is no good to anyone, it can get you killed." He said as he tossed it down beside him along with the belt.

Reaching over to retrieve his bag of jerky and tying it on. "Ain't got time to bury you, but you will be buried nice and deep as those that follow will take care of that," Gray Wolf said as he mounted up. Reluctantly, the horses moved out. Slowly, he headed out and got back on his trail.

CHAPTER SIX

Gray Wolf rode until the midday sun and only then did he stop to let his horses rest and graze as he ate a little deer jerky and cooled down under the shade of a rock overhang. Watching his back trail as he sat back, he did not think those who followed would be back more than a half hour. After giving his mounts time to eat a few mouthfuls of grass and drink from a small pool of water, he remounted and pushed on. It was not long before he came across an old tree, he had seen it few times sitting in the middle of the trail. This scrub oak had died long ago leaving its large dried trunk and the pieces that fall from it made a good fire. But this time he could not stop to enjoy a cup of coffee, to pressed for time the Pawnee was pushing him and he had no idea how far back they were.

Stopping to think, "I have been running long enough. Pawnee, you have been pushing me and I have about had enough," he said to no one. "You and them army boys it's getting about time to make a stand and this is as a good a place as any. Make you think that anyway." Looking back, he could see a good mile out now that he was starting to reach a higher elevation. Here he had rocks and the old oak to hide behind. He had plans of riding on, he had been riding seems like forever and that ole army dog won't break the trail. *Maybe it is time to do it for him. A bullet in that thick head of the sergeant might help to end this.*

Looking around, he found a little pool of water behind a large rock not far from the trail with enough grass to last the horses a good day. Staking them out behind the rock to protect them from flying bullets. He had dropped his saddle and supplies behind the tree. Taking out his rifle, a Winchester, called by most 'old yellow', he had found by a tent and liberated it from one of the boys sleeping as he did almost all of his supplied. He sat up camp, built a fire and put the coffee on, complete with a piece of ham he had taken from the line upon leaving.

"One thing is for sure," he whispered to himself as he poured a cup of coffee, "graves will be dug here. Me or them, not running any more you ole boot licker Pawnee will join me if I am to be buried here. We just might go hunting together in that great happy hunting ground."

It was after he was done eating and he was on his third cup of coffee, he spotted movement a good mile out. Riders, a wagon, and dust flying. Watching and waiting for them to come into range, Gray Wolf packed up his eating supplies and kicked his fire out. By that time, they had come in within a good half mile. Hiding behind the tree to keep the Pawnee from spotting him, but he would have bet a dollar to a Johnny cake he already had.

As he waited, he watched them come to a stop and dismount. Straining his eyes, he could not find that Pawnee anywhere. Sitting on his saddle leaning against the tree as he held his rifle close, he rolled himself a smoke; something he did not do much, never had the habit, but he had time. Pulling out the string bag as he held his paper tight. Pouring in a generous amount, before rolling and sealing it with a lick. Looking around as he struck a match to light it and as he puffed it to get it lit a voice called out. "Kiowa what are you up to?" It was that Pawnee; he had somehow bellied up and did it unseen.

Standing up, Gray Wolf looked around, but did not see him. It sounding like he was a ways out as he called. "Pawnee where are you at? You crawling like a snake, no way you walked up here. Tired of you bellying up on me It's time for us to finish this and be about our business."

"Gray Wolf, you're loco. I don't have to belly nowhere, you blind Kiowa. I could have ridden up here on a wagon full of burning coal dust. But you ain't going to live long if you keep this up. The sergeant has eight men down there and they are as ready to finish this as he is. Believe me, they are ready to get back to the line where they have tents to sleep in. You have a tent to sleep in, hot grub, and warm cot. I don't think so, but you will have a warm hole if you don't get a move on. The sergeant will be sure of that Kiowa. It is a hanging he wants. That old tree there will suit him just fine, bury you at the root of it. No Gray Wolf, this is not the time or the place. He is spit fire mad about you painting his face, stealing his boots, and spending his boot monies. You really want me to report back you are going to make your last stand here?"

"I don't care what you tell him, that horse shooter, but I am here to stay and here I am!" Gray Wolf screamed as he took a shot out at nothing.

"What are you shooting at you loony Kiowa?"

"Come out and I will show you, like I said, it is time to end this, makes no differences to me. My old carcass or yours, it's time to end this. Pawnee why don't you go home and leave them to me? You have done your job, there is no need to fertilize this old tree with your rotting hide. The sergeant will be buried here, no need in your carcass feeding it as well. Now belly your way back and let him take the reins and saddle off of you, put you out to graze. I can handle him. You hear me Pawnee?"

Gray Wolf waited, but no answer came. After a few minutes, he saw him walk back into their area as they had not made camp yet. But as soon as he got back, he could see them unsaddling the horses and smoke coming up from most likely Deeds getting the noon day meal and coffee on. Sitting there, he figured that in about an hour he could expect them to start riding in after they had rested and ate their meal. Gray Wolf sat watching and laughed as he considered that Pawnee reporting that he was going to hold them off and fight him and his men using only an old falling apart oak tree for a shield.

Now that he had them off-guard, he could ease on out and leave them, but first things first. He quickly saddled up the horse's unseen behind the rocks as he knew most likely he was being watch by the sergeant and he would be using that spy glass. The thing could see the buttons on a man's shirt from a mile out, or he was told as he had never used one himself. But it did not matter what was unseen is unseen. *I am going to get you and that Army Dog off my tracks. You have been pushing me far too long and nobody does this to me for long. My haybale must be falling apart with me talking to my horse.* "You think so Mister Rabbit? No matter, we are going to move uphill a way and I am going to get that Army dog off our trail and then we can go on or go back. Maybe I'll spend the remaining amount of the gold in my new boots. Maybe get you some a bag of oaks too. You'd like that huh Mister Rabbit? A clean stable and a good rub down with a belly full of oaks. Maybe we talk of this latter Mister Rabbit, I have something to take care of right now," Gray Wolf said as he turned and headed back out to the old oak.

Holding his rifle up like he waited for them, Gray Wolf propped it up and eased back behind it. He was about to move out behind the rocks as he spotted a white flag and that blasted sergeant headed up the hill. Taking his rifle back in hand. He Watched him slowly walk up as he aimed his rifle straight at his head.

"You know Sergeant, you have been pushing me and I am tired of it. What you say we end this; I put some lead into that thick skull of yours?" Gray Wolf said as he got close.

"Listen here Kiowa, you have left the line and I am ordering you to return. I give you my word you will not be harmed on your prompt return. But you must turn in the supplies, horses, and guns you have taken. And return my boots and anything left in them. This is your last chance, after this, if you don't give yourself up, I will hang you on the spot."

"Hang me, seems to me you are in the wrong place to be talking about hanging. No way up that hill, but the path you have just taken, I will shoot any that try and I am holding the high ground here." Gray Wolf said as he aimed his rifle at his forehead. "You will have to admit I have had the chance many times to finish this and I have let you go. Why you should ask? I am growing tired of this game. Gray Wolf, I say to myself, why don't I finish this and trim them long ears of the sergeant? Maybe some lead in that thick head would bring a little sense to him. But no, I wait. For now, anyway. But I can change my mind anytime now as I am tired of being the good little Indian here. Sergeant, I am a Kiowa, a proud Kiowa and starting right here, I am declaring war on you and your little army. Especially that Pawnee dog, I am going to give you time just to show you I am not all bad to make it back down to your camp before I start returning your bullets, one at a time. But know this, I am going to kill you and that Pawnee first, before I go after any of your remaining men who don't turn back and leave this old Kiowa to himself. I didn't start this; I was minding my own business when your men rode into our camp and started pushing us out. Yes, that old chief signed a peace treaty, Sergeant, I didn't."

"You are going to regret this Indian. It was your last chance to leave this place alive. Now you won't leave it, you'll be buried here. All I have to do is motion for my men and you..."

"Go ahead and motion for them and you will lose the top of your head to this Buffalo rifle. Love these army rifles, in the right hands a man can drop a bull at three hundred yards and 30 feet, well there won't be enough left of you to make a good burial. Now Sergeant, there going to be a hole wide enough to drive a mule team through. You sure you want to do that? Now why don't you come on up here and join old Gray Wolf? What are you going to do with me? Well, you see I am a thinking about that and I ain't decided yet. You know they say my people back before the white men came here, ate their enemies and took their spirit away from them by eating their liver, heart, or tongue. You got an awful lot of tongue there Sergeant; them big ears of yours could use a shorting, or that cold heart of yours could use a little warming up in a roasting fire. Then again, could just let you go if you would leave me be. I am going up into those hills and their ain't nobody going to be hearing from me. Now turn around and keep your hands up." As he did, Gray Wolf popped him on the head with his rifle butt sending him crashing to the ground. "Well, that should hold you for a spell," he said as he walked off.

Walking away and getting on his horse, Gray Wolf laughed for the next half hour thinking about scaring the wits out of that old sergeant. Riding steady and slow as now he was headed up and it would not be long before he vanished into those approaching hills. Dark would come early to these mountain trails. Most likely after the sergeant woke up and got back to his men, he would be too late for him to start out giving Gray Wolf a little more time.

CHAPTER SEVEN

Waking up as he looked up at White Hawk. "Sergeant, why are you napping here in the late afternoon?"

"Napping, that blasted bloodthirsty Kiowa hit me in my living quarters. I have no idea how long I been out up here."

"Not that long Sergeant, when you didn't come back, I came to check on you."

"Have you seen him anywhere around?"

"No Sergeant, he has packed up and left, and not much daylight left. It'll be dark soon up here."

"I guess he got a jump on us, that was his plan all along I would bet. Well come first light White Hawk, we are going to hit the gate running." The sergeant said as he stood up and brushed the dirt off.

Walking back to camp, the sergeant and White Hawk talked about the possible places he could have gone. Which was just about anywhere.

"Why do you think he didn't just finish the job and blow my fool head off for thinking I could reason with that renegade?"

"Sergeant, it would be my guess, he just wants to vanish without having someone trailing him for murder. He has already shot one, but to add a Sergeant of the U.S.

Army to it, they wouldn't ever let him get any rest. As it is, they just might grow tired of following a cold trail and let him be."

"Well, I have to tell you White Hawk, it is starting to cross my mind. But no one Kiowa is going to get the best of this old sergeant, been in this man's Army for 25 years now and I plan to retire soon and I don't need one crazy Kiowa staining my record. You boys got the coffee on?" the sergeant asked as they walked back into camp.

"Yes Sir, Sergeant," Wagon Master Thomas replied as he poured a cup and handed it to him. "You look kind of weak on your legs Sarge you, okay?" Private Thomas asked.

"Yes, I will be okay, mountain air getting to me," the sergeant responded. Sitting down as night rolled in fast as it does in the high mountain area with the sun being blocked in late afternoon. Sitting around the fire telling stories of past battles, old girlfriends, and family back home kept the men busy as the sergeant rolled over and fell asleep.

White Hawk eased out into the night and looked up into the higher elevations to see if there was any light flickering from a fire. There was, it looked to be five hundred feet up and a mile or more out. That Kiowa had managed to keep two steps ahead and he just might break loose and make it to the freedom of those high hills and who's to say he hasn't already. He just might be the one that got away. Smiling, White Hawk walked back into camp and laid down and it wasn't long before he was sound asleep dreaming of when the forest was thick with deer, bear, and quail.

Hours later, he was awakened by the sound of the fire popping as one of the watchers laid more sticks onto the fire. "What time is it?" he whispered to Private Colts.

Pulling out his pocket watch and looking at it as he held it down by the fire to see the time. "Half past five," he answered, "and the moon never came up. It's been a dark one this night. If you a mind to get up, won't hurt my feeling none. I been as jittery as June bug sitting next to a hungry frog."

"Why is that?" White Hawk asked as he sat up.

"That Kiowa has already made a fool out of me twice; I was on guard duty two of the times he snuck in here. There ain't a going to be no next time, I'm going to cut him for all of the jawing I got from the sergeant. That blame fool ain't a going to do it again."

"No Private, I don't think you have anything to worry about tonight; his fire burns high up in the hills, he's not close. Tomorrow night might be altogether different. The sarge is burning with rage to catch him, that knot on his head is going to hurt in that bright sun."

"You bet your boots I am," the sergeant said as he sat up and rubbed his head. "It hurts like the dickens and I am going to get that waylaying Kiowa."

Looking around, Deeds had a fire going and the coffee was hot outside of camp. "Alright Boys, wake up and get some vittles in your bellies; we're getting an early start as soon as the sun is peeping through, we are moving out."

An hour later, they were back on the trail except Deeds which had to turn around and head back to the line as the trail was too narrow as it went up into the mountain as it grew narrow and winding. White Hawk followed the tracks out of habit, but there was only one way and that was up.

Scanning the upper areas for falling rocks, an ambush, or a blocked path. There were a couple of times the sergeant thought he saw movement. He was sure he had glanced Gray Wolf on the trail above them. White Hawk noticed it as well. He was surprised the sergeant had not wasted a shot. It was too far out, for now anyway. Over the next hour, they moved slow as they gently headed up and as he was about to suggest a break as a shot rang out as it echoed across the hills. Looking around, it was Private Thomas having chanced a shot.

"What are you shooting at!" the sergeant yelled, "I haven't seen anything?"

"I hit him, winged him!" he screamed out; "I slowed him down."

Private, if you did, we'll get him now, follow the blood trail. But no more shooting unless I give the word;

there are a lot of loose rocks up there and a shot could bring it down on top of us."

Looking up, White Hawk did not see Gray Wolf or his horses, didn't mean anything. If he was hit, he would have moved back closer to the trail wall. Problem is, if he is hit now, he will be blocking the trail. He will fight to his last bullet. The sergeant may be right if he did wing him, he had not seen anything, but at the time he was focused on not falling over the side or letting a rock from above hit him. Not trusting Gray Wolf not to roll rocks onto them. Unlike Gray Wolf, he did not know much about these mountains; his people always stayed clear of them. Nothing here except sheep and goats, their hides were good for the winter chill, but deer leather was more plentiful and easier to get. Buffalo, back when there was buffalo made better blankets.

The sergeant was pushing now, carelessly ready to fall into another of Gray Wolf's traps. Seems he would have learned by now, that one had a bag of tricks. White Hawk held back as the sergeant rushed ahead and took his men with him leaving him behind as he stepped aside and let them go. *Going back to the line alone seemed highly likely at this point. Then again, this game could be over and Gray Wolf could get them all. Just might spend a few days up here and learn a few things about these mountains or face that Kiowa myself* he thought as he looked around at the mountain peaks.

A few minutes later, White Hawk heard shots being fired and it seemed to be coming from a rifle and not the pistols used by most of the troopers. The sergeant would have at close range used his pistol as would have his men. It had to be Gray Wolf blocking the trail. Running to catch up as he spotted the horses coming back down without their riders, blocking the trail as he managed to head them off and secure them to a rope between two boulders. Before heading on up, White Hawk was out of breath by the time he reached the bend only to find the troopers pinned against the wall and the sergeant was wounded and hiding behind a rock bleeding heavy from his neck.

All his men were okay, using the trail wall and rocks for cover trying to find a way to get to the sergeant and drag him back to the safety of the rock face pushing off in the bend in the trail. The sergeant had rushed a head thinking he would find Gray Wolf face down on the trail. Now he was wounded, and could not move as Gray Wolf bounced bullets around him any time he tried to move back. They were pinned down, no way to go ahead and no way back as any that tried would be left out in the open to Gray Wolf's mercy. Mercy, not from that Kiowa. This trail will be flowing with blood before this is over.

Looking around, White Hawk spotted a tree growing out from the above trail only a dozen feet or so over them. If he could toss a rope over it, he just might be able to climb up and change this to his advantage. But the ropes were on the horses and they were back down the trail.

"A fine fix we are in here," Private Thomas said as he watched White Hawk look around. "I can't even stick my head out to get a shot off, That Kiowa is in a prime position. He doesn't look to be wounded from what I seen either," he complained.

"Not likely to be, he tricked you and the sergeant again."

"White Hawk that Kiowa is going to be the death of us all. Blazes, I say we leave this place and let him be. He can have these rocks and goats."

White Hawk nodded his head in agreement. "You could be right Private," he responded as he pointed to the sergeant that was not moving. "Thomas, I think your sergeant is dead, looks to be anyway. He's not moving, who is in charge now?"

"I guess that would be me as I have been bumped down for fighting and drinking so many times, I joined up a year before the sergeant. The men follow me anyway."

"What was your rank?"

"Lieutenant, the first time and Sergeant, the second time. Private, the other times.

"Well Private, Lieutenant, Sergeant Thomas, you might get your rank back after this, so in the order of things, let's save time here and jump ahead. Sergeant, Lieutenant Thomas, what do you suggest we do here? We can't advance as he blocks the trail and holds a higher advantage, we can't retreat or he will cut us to pieces, we could sit here until dark and might be able if there is no moon tonight sneak out."

"Hawk, I like it here, no hurry, but up would be my thought. The other trail isn't that much higher," he said as he pointed up.

"Yes, you are right, but you are forgetting we have no rope and the horses with the rope is down the trail aways." About that time, a few small rocks fell from above. Looking up in time to see Gray Wolf above ride out of sight.

"Private Jones, get the horses that are tied down trail!" Thomas screamed as he ran out to check on the sergeant. "Dead," he said as he checked for any breath.

"Okay, Sergeant Thomas, are we going to follow that Kiowa up and let him pick us off one at a time or turn back and report that he got away? The captain ain't going to like it if you turn back and less so if you get his men killed."

"Hawk, is there any way around this trail? A back way to cut him off?"

"I have no idea, never hunted here and that Kiowa knows these hills like the back of his hand. Like I told the sergeant, it would be suicide to try and follow him up here. One thing I can say is, if you do decide to follow him up, is take it slow, that Kiowa will ambush you killing one at a time. This trail will flow with blood. Killing the sergeant is only the beginning."

"Then you are advising me to let him ride off and surrender to one Kiowa?"

"Surrender? I think it's more of an ordered retreat in the face of an unwinnable circumstance. No, let him live and at the same time, let your men see another day."

It was at that time a shot rang out and hit the rocks between Private Thomas and White Hawk. Looking up to see where it had come from, "Sergeant, I think it just went from an ordered retreat to a fall back under decisive firepower." What Hawk said as he spotted Gray Wolf above them and he had worked his way around the upper elevation and was now in front with a clear shot. Holding his fire as he could easily drop each one, but didn't as he watched and waited to see what they would do.

"Drop your gun Thomas," White Hawk said as he dropped his and each man did the same. "See what I mean Sergeant Thomas, he knows too much about this area to trap him."

"Trap him, now we can't even hold to the rocks."

"Then are you breaking this trail here?"

"Yes, we are turning back. What is one Kiowa anyway. I am sure we lost a few along the way."

"Kiowa, you have won, we are turning back and I will not be on your trail tomorrow!" White Hawk screamed as he waved his flat right hand forward. A sigh to go in peace

Smiling, Gray Wolf slowly eased back out of sight.

CHAPTER EIGHT

Days later, Private Thomas caught back up with the line and reported to Captain Lane that the Kiowa gave them the slip as he made his way into the higher mountains, an area he knew well. Also, they had brought Sergeant Mason's body back for burial as he died in battle trying to apprehend a crazed renegade.

Over the next three years there were reports of a lone Kiowa up in the mountains. Reported by hunters and trappers that he had been seen living quietly trading furs, meat, and sometimes playing tricks on these traveling through the lonely mountain trail. It was said you could hear him laughing for miles away in the confines of the valley walls. One miner reported of having woke up to him standing over him as he slept.